INSIDE

Inside

Bill Carey

Lighthouse

CONTENTS

FOREWORD

One night I had a dream... That's where this story begins. It was Houston, Texas in 1983. It had been a very ordinary day. I went to bed, and had a most extraordinary dream. When I awoke, I had lived ten years in the lives of an entire town of people. I knew all their names, what streets they lived on, and even the history of their people. I knew them as intimately as my own family, and my attachment to them was just that strong.

The sense of loss when I awoke and realized that none of those people were real was immense. I had to find some way to make them live again. And so, over the course of several years, I wrote down the story. Perhaps on the pages of this book, Michael London and the people of Inside will find some immortality. Michael, this is for you.

INSIDE TOWN MAP

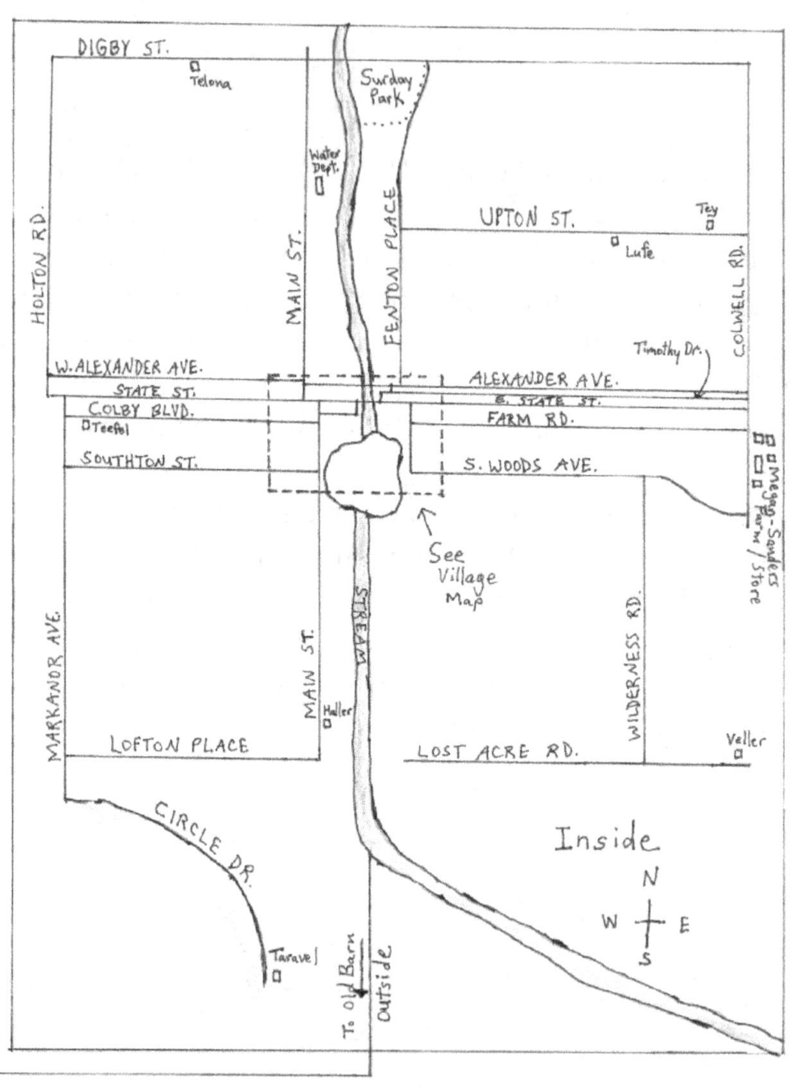

INSIDE VILLAGE MAP

1

JEREMY

Michael rolled over and looked at the clock. The numbers glared mercilessly back at him: 2:48 a.m. Two minutes later than the last time he looked. It couldn't be only two minutes, he thought, as he reached for the clock and held it next to his ear. It was warm against his skin, and hummed gently. Satisfied that the clock was working properly, he replaced the offending device on the nightstand.

Outside, the rain had slowed to a small deluge. The night sounds of the city seemed to intensify in the rain: car horns, a distant siren, and music from the bar down the street. A few blocks away, a dog was barking. As if to complete his aria, the dog began to howl, and an icy chill ran down Michael's spine.

What was it Cousin Jenny had said about a dog howling at night? His mind went back to his ninth birthday, when Cousin Jenny, eight years his senior, had entertained the kids with ghost stories. He could hear her voice now as plainly as if she had been right there in his bedroom: "Every time a dog howls at night, it means someone is going to die." He knew she hadn't been serious. She was only trying to scare the younger kids. Her words had stayed with him, though, and now loomed larger than life as the dog howled again.

Michael thought of Jeremy, lying in the hospital with tubes in his nose and needles stuck into every available vein. No! He isn't going to die! Every synapse in his brain screamed denial. No! Michael wrestled with himself for control of his thoughts. Once again, the dog howled, and Michael bolted upright in his bed. He was drenched with perspiration, and struggled to catch his breath. "No," he screamed, still gasping for air. "No!" As he sat up in bed panting, he began to think he had been dreaming. The dream was over now. There was no dog. Jeremy wasn't dying. Michael's brain registered these thoughts, and his mind continued: I'll just reach over to the right side of the bed, to Jeremy's side, and he'll be there. I'll just reach over and put my arms around him. He paused in his thoughts, as his mind grasped for some thread of truth he felt was eluding him. I'll just reach over... His body didn't move. What was it he was trying to remember? And why was he afraid to look for Jeremy? No, it wasn't a dream. The dog howled again, and Michael remembered.

"Happy anniversary, Jeremy!"

Jeremy's face went pale as he stopped in the doorway. Had he forgotten their anniversary? His mind began to search lamely for an excuse, as Michael stood grinning at him. But no excuse would come. His mind a blank, he stood in the door-way with his mouth hanging open. After a moment, his brain slipped into gear, and he remembered that it wasn't their anniversary. Michael, however, was already on the floor, convulsed with laughter.

"You jerk," was all Jeremy could think of to say, and then he, too, began to laugh.

"You should have seen your face," Michael said, as he rolled on the floor holding his stomach. His sides ached from laughing, and tears rolled off his cheeks. "You were nearly incontinent!"

"Yeah, very funny, Michael. What's the deal here?"

Michael, breathless, stood up, and wiped his face with his hand. "It's our anniversary," he said. "Two years and four months."

"Two years and four months," Jeremy repeated blankly, as if the words were in a foreign tongue. "Are you out of your mind?" he asked, finally comprehending Michael's words.

"No, I'm just in love with the most wonderful man in the world."

"Well, don't let *me* find out about him!" Jeremy teased. Michael laughed and hugged him.

The call had come in the late afternoon. Jeremy was at work. He often had to work weekends, and that particular Saturday he had been called in early. Michael used the free time to catch up on grocery shopping. Later, he walked up to 86th Street. Brooklyn has many good places to shop, but 86th Street was Michael's favorite. There were so many stores, and he loved them all. He stopped for lunch at a Chinese restaurant, a rare treat for him. He and Jeremy never ate Chinese together, because, as Jeremy was fond of saying, "It looks like it's already been eaten!"

By the time Michael got home, loaded with packages, it was well past four thirty. Jeremy was usually home by four. But even as he turned from Fort Hamilton Parkway onto 72nd Street, Michael could see that Jeremy's car wasn't in the driveway yet. As he entered the hallway, Michael tripped, falling headfirst into his packages. He muttered under his breath, annoyed at his own clumsiness, gathered his packages and walked to the kitchen, dumping them unceremoniously on the table. He let himself fall into a chair and closed his eyes, feeling the need for a short nap. About four years should do it, he thought.

The ringing of the telephone summoned his thoughts from whatever far-off place they were about to wander. He hoped it would stop, but finally reached for it on the tenth ring.

"Hello," he muttered grumpily into the phone, annoyed at having been disturbed.

"Michael London?" queried a crisp, female voice at the other end.

"Yeah?"

"One moment please."

"Michael?" It was Jim, Jeremy's boss.

Jeremy probably has to work late again, he thought. Why can't they ever let him have some time to himself?

"Michael, Jeremy's in the hospital."

"Jim, what happened? Is he all right?"

"He collapsed at work. They don't know why yet. We couldn't wake him up. He's at Maimonides, room 862. I'll stay until you get here."

His mind a blank, Michael held the phone to his ear, as if the disconnected instrument might still give him some vital piece of information about Jeremy. Then, jumping to his feet, he threw the receiver in the general direction of the wall and ran next door.

"Laura," he shouted, as he pounded on her door. Her eye appeared in the peephole, and Michael said, "Jeremy's in the hospital. Can I use your car?"

The door flew open and she said, "I'll go with you," running ahead of him to the car.

Michael pushed back the blanket and turned to look at the clock again: Four thirty. He must have slept. The phone had woken him. It continued to ring, as he looked apprehensively at its dim outline on the nightstand. His hand shook as he lifted the receiver and held it to his ear.

"He--Hello?"

"Mr. London? This is Dr. Chang. It's time."

He hung up the phone, then picked it up again and dialed Laura's number.

"Hello?" Laura answered, still mostly asleep. "Hello?" she said again. "Michael, is that you? Don't move! I'll be right there!" She hung up.

Michael sat on the edge of the bed, holding the receiver on his knees. Laura let herself in and came into the bedroom. Taking the phone from him, she helped him to dress: "Put your arm in here. Put your foot in." He numbly complied with her instructions.

When they arrived at the hospital, Dr. Chang met them at the nurses' station. "I'm glad you could get here so quickly," she said. "It won't be long now. You can both go in."

As they entered the room, Laura wondered if perhaps they weren't too late. Jeremy's skin was a dusky shade of gray. His eyes, partly open, were sunken and unseeing. Only the weak sound that came from his white, chapped lips betrayed him as alive.

"Mom?" he asked, "Is Dad . . ." His voice trailed off.

"Jeremy, it's Michael."

"Michael? Michael? Are you here? It hurts, Michael. It hurts." Even though the nurses regularly injected mega-doses of drugs into him, they couldn't kill the pain. "It's so dark in here. Mom? Can you turn on the light?"

"Jeremy, can you hear me? It's Michael."

"Yes, Michael. Did I tell you? I'm sick, Michael."

"Yes, I know, Baby."

"Michael, I'm gonna die. I'm sorry. I'm sorry. I didn't mean to, Mom. It was an accident." As Jeremy continued to speak to his long-dead mother, Michael and Laura held to each other, afraid. As they watched, a sound came from deep inside of Jeremy: a groan, then a horrible gurgling. "Michael," he whispered, as blood began to flow from his nose and mouth. A machine next to the bed began to wail, as if in mortal agony. Laura and Michael still clung to each other, and Laura began to sob. As the room filled with nurses, they were propelled into the hallway and left alone. There they stood for what seemed an eternity. Michael wanted so much to cry, but he couldn't. There was a lump in his throat, but no tears would come. His chest, wet with Laura's tears, ached. As they stood there, he wondered if perhaps it had been he, himself, who had just died.

2

PULLING UP STAKES

The funeral was a nightmare. Jeremy's sister, Lena, blamed Michael for her brother's death. Her husband Terry tried to keep her civil, but to no avail. She created a scene at the funeral home, telling everyone that Michael had given her brother AIDS. The fact that Jeremy had not died of AIDS, and had, in fact, tested negative for exposure to the virus, meant nothing to her. She hated Michael, and she made sure everyone knew it.

If her actions at the wake were in poor taste, they were nothing at all in comparison to her behavior at the church. "You miserable queer!" she screamed, leaping from her seat and pointing at Michael. "You did this to him! First you turned him into a faggot, and then you killed him. You killed my brother!"

Terry took her by the arm and led her outside to their car. That evening, he telephoned Michael to apologize for the morning's events. "I wish I could say that she didn't mean what she said. I know how much you loved Jeremy, and how much her words this morning must have hurt. I'm really sorry, Michael."

"Thanks. I don't hold anything she said against her. I know she loved Jeremy, too."

There was a brief pause in the conversation, and then Terry said, "Michael, I have to ask you something. I hate to bring it up now, but it's important. Did Jeremy have a will?"

"A will? No, why? Did Lena tell you to ask?"

"No!" Terry answered quickly. "Lena would kill me if she even knew I was talking to you. It's because of your house. It's in Jeremy's name, and Lena wants it. She went to see a lawyer this afternoon. He said that if Jeremy didn't leave a will specifically naming you to inherit the house, then in the eyes of the law, you don't exist. I'm sorry to have to hit you with this right now, but I was worried about you."

"There is no will, Terry. Neither of us ever got around to writing one. There didn't seem to be any hurry. We didn't know he was sick until it was too late."

"What will you do, then?" Terry asked.

"I don't know. I'm too tired to think right now. I've got to get some sleep."

"OK, Michael. I'll call you tomorrow.

"Thanks, Terry. Good night."

Michael slept fitfully that night. His dreams were a blur of Jeremy's death, Lena screaming, "You miserable queer, you killed him," and Terry saying, "In the eyes of the law, you don't exist." The dreams seemed interminable. Then, in a rare display of mercy, the alarm clock woke him at six o'clock. Even though his body insisted that it hadn't been to bed yet, his mind forced him to get up, being unwilling to face the prospect of another nightmare.

The nightmares didn't end, though. As he started on his way to work, the voices of Lena, Terry, Dr. Chang and Jeremy all ran together in his mind, and he got on the wrong train. An hour late for work, he sat down at his desk. The voices in his head were now indistinguishable from each other, a roar, like the sea, or a crowded subway platform. Stacks of papers remained untouched on the desk. The computer terminal flashed endless lines of data in vain. The phone rang unanswered.

"London! London!" Michael looked up dazedly. His supervisor, Mr. Thomas, was leaning over the desk. "I have been standing here, Michael London, for the last five minutes. What's the matter with you? Are you drunk? I told you at ten thirty that I wanted the data for the Sherman account within an hour. It is now one fifteen, and the Sherman data is nowhere in sight. Now what is the problem?"

Michael did not respond. There was simply too much pressure. Lena's lawyer had phoned that morning to give him a deadline to move out of the house. He had no place to go. Laura was moving back to Schenectady to take care of her mother. Jeremy was dead, and now, who is this man standing here yelling?

"London, are you listening to me? London! Where are you going? Answer me! If you walk out that door, don't bother to come back! What are all you people staring at? Get back to work!"

Michael heard only a faraway buzz. *Jeremy's dead. Laura's going to Schenectady. Deadline to move. Jeremy's dead. Jeremy.* As the elevator doors closed, his thoughts filled with Jeremy, and for all too brief a moment, he managed to forget that Jeremy was gone. But when he arrived at the empty house, the house that was no longer his home, cruel truth restored the painful memory.

He did it: Somehow, he had squeezed every piece of clothing he owned into two suitcases. After adding toiletries, some books, his photo album, and a few odds and ends, it was truly a miracle that the suitcases ever closed. He packed mechanically, without emotion. He was going home. To what, he wasn't sure. His only family was Cousin Jenny in Philadelphia, whose husband hated gay people. He couldn't go there. So he was going home.

He had no illusions about it: He knew Coalmont, Tennessee wouldn't roll out any red carpets for him. He was last there three years ago, after fire destroyed his boyhood home, trapping his parents inside. Some of the neighbors had been openly hostile toward Michael back then when he arrived to make burial arrangements. They didn't like him then, and he knew they wouldn't like him now.

No, he had no illusions about it: Coalmont wasn't a bad place, but it definitely was not New York or San Francisco. Then why was he going back? He wasn't sure. Perhaps, he thought, it's an instinct. A hurt child instinctively seeks for home. And he was hurting. Perhaps, then, it was that hurt that pushed him to return to Tennessee.

Michael walked through the Port Authority bus terminal oblivious to his surroundings. Neither the most fervent converts of Reverend Moon, nor the most dedicated chanters of Hare Krishna were able to distract him from his void.

In his haste to board his bus, he nearly trampled a tall person of indiscernible gender who was wearing a white robe and holding a stack of pamphlets written in something that definitely was not English. Muttering an epithet, the figure rose to his feet and proceeded to address Michael's retreating form using highly colorful words that definitely *were* English.

Sitting in the back of the bus, Michael waited impatiently for the driver to board. Right now, nothing mattered as much as getting out of New York. If he could get out of New York, maybe he could get away from the memories: Lena, Mr. Thomas, and Dr. Chang. Laura was gone. Jeremy's dead. He might leave behind Lena and the others, but he knew Jeremy's ghost would follow. Whenever he tried to sleep, he heard

Jeremy. When he watched TV, every face was Jeremy's. Even on the subway, Jeremy was there. Once, he even called out to someone who looked like Jeremy from the back. But it wasn't him. Jeremy's dead. Jeremy, who had always been so strong for him. Why can't I be strong for him now? Michael thought.

As the bus pulled out into the Manhattan night, a scared little boy named Michael shivered in the back, and fought to keep back the tears.

3

GOING HOME

After two days, the bus pulled into McMinnville, Tennessee. Bottom sore, and limbs aching from disuse, Michael emerged from the bus. He reclaimed his luggage from underneath, and headed south on Route 56. Hitching a ride as far as Beersheba Springs, he then started walking south again.

It had begun to rain, making him very wet, very fast. Just beyond the junction of Routes 56 and 108, he got another ride. Tossing his bags into the back seat, he sat in front, sloshing loudly as he did so.

"Sorry about getting your seat wet," he apologized.

The older man, taking a sip of hot coffee, replied, "S'all right. Can't help the weather. How far ya headed?"

"Coalmont."

"You from there?" the man asked.

"Yeah, born and raised there," Michael said.

"You been away a while, though, ain't ya? Been livin' out of state?"

"Yeah," Michael said, both surprised and amused. "How can you tell?"

"Wasn't hard to figure out," the man replied, but offered no explanation.

As they drove through Coalmont, Michael realized that the man was expecting him to say where he wanted to get out. Truthfully, he didn't know where to get out. There was no one in Coalmont who would help him. Not sure what to do, he said nothing.

"If you don't get out soon," the man said, "you'll be in Tracy City. You goin' to Coalmont, or ain'tcha?"

"Yes. This will be fine right here." Pulling his bags out of the car, he said, "Thank you," and closed the door. Michael waved as the car pulled away. The man didn't wave back.

Michael turned and looked around, wondering where to go. He was on the south side of town, on Route 56, but in an area with few houses. This he counted a blessing, not being in any hurry to meet up with the local people. He decided to leave the main road. There was a side road, heading east, and for lack of a better plan, Michael took it. The rain had stopped, but he was still wet, and very uncomfortable.

About five miles east of the main road was a dirt road that headed south. At first, Michael passed it by, but then, for no reason he was aware of, he went back and took it. The rain had turned the road to mud, making the walk difficult.

As he walked, he listened to the thunder. It seemed to follow him, like a faraway voice, saying things he didn't want to hear: *"You're alone. Jeremy's dead. Laura's gone. You're alone. You're alone."* His stomach felt deep and empty, yet he wasn't hungry. *"You're alone. No home. No home. Jeremy's dead."* The thunder tormented him with its omniscience. It was getting darker. Michael realized that night was falling and he had no place to sleep. *"No home, no home,"* the thunder sang. *"No home. You're alone. Jeremy's dead."*

He walked on, as the maddening voice of the sky confronted him with painful truth. Night came quickly. As the light disappeared from the heavens, the night world came alive with the many sounds of the woods. An owl? A raccoon? He couldn't tell. But each creature of the woods, as it awoke, joined in the song of the thunder, until all of nature tormented him in unison: *"No home. No home. You're alone and Jeremy's dead. Jeremy's dead. Jeremy's dead. No home."*

Michael started to cry as he walked in the dark. It didn't matter. The dark didn't care if he cried, did it? Was the dark singing the awful song, too? Dropping his suitcases, he fell to his knees and bent over to the muddy road. Around him, the chorus increased in volume and fervor: *"You're alone! No home! Jeremy's dead! Jeremy's dead! Jeremy's dead!"*

Then Michael's own voice pierced the din. "Jeremy!" he screamed, lifting his face and his voice to the sky. "Jeremy! I need you! Where are you? Jeremy!"

But his only answer was from nature, which continued to mock him: *"Jeremy's dead! Can't come back! You're alone! No home! Jeremy's dead!"* Michael lay in the mud, sobbing, listening to the chant: *"Jeremy's dead! Can't come back!"*

"Michael!" There was silence. The singing had stopped. All the night was still. Had he imagined it? "Michael!"

There it was again! Someone was calling him. A woman's voice was calling to him. Somehow, she had made the torment stop. The horrible song was over.

"Michael!"

He looked up and saw her looking down at him. The moon had appeared, and he saw her clearly in its light. She wore a long, dark skirt, and a white blouse with a brooch, Vic-torian style. Her hair was piled up on her head, and gathered in a bun, in the fashion popular among ladies of the nineteenth century. Even with only the moon for light, he could tell that her hair was a brilliant shade of red. Her facial features, outlined in moonlight, were exquisite. She was smiling.

"Michael, are you all right?"

Michael, very frightened, looked at her as though he were seeing a heavenly vision, for indeed, it had crossed his mind that he had died, and that this beautiful creature was an angel.

"I asked if you were all right. Can you hear me?"

"Yes. I'm . . . I'm sorry. You scared me. I'm OK, I guess. Who are you? How do you know my name?

She smiled again. "My name is Emily Grae. I know a lot about you, Michael. I was sent to get you."

Michael's hands went up to cover his face. From behind them, he spoke. "Then I *am* dead!"

"Dead?!" she answered rather loudly. "Whatever gave you the idea that you're dead?"

"Then I'm not dead?"

"No, you silly goose, you're very much alive! I've come to take you Inside. The Seers will be able to help you. They told me about Jeremy. I'm very sorry."

"You know about Jeremy? Wait a minute, who are the Seers? And you've come to take me inside what?"

"I know this is difficult for you to understand," she said, smiling, "but you must come Inside with me. You see, your destiny is Inside. It is rather strange, for you are an Outsider, but the Seers said it was meant to be. I know you don't under-stand now, but come with me, and I'll take you Inside. You're cold and wet; you need to get into some dry clothes. In the morning, the Seers will explain everything."

Too shaken to object, Michael let her lead him to the side of the road. They headed toward an old barn that looked like the next good wind would topple it into oblivion. Instead of going into the barn, though, she walked to the left side of the build-ing. There was a narrow path, perhaps two feet wide, between the barn and the woods. The trees bore signs forbidding tres-passers to set foot in their realm, and Michael wondered who owned the land. Behind the barn was a muddy path, five feet wide at best, leading far into the woods. Emily moved silently down the path, and Michael numbly followed, his mind a blur.

4

INSIDE

The mud made walking difficult for Michael. It seemed to pose no problem for his mysterious escort, however. She glided on the path as though it were a frozen stream and she a figure skater. As they moved, Michael tried to collect his thoughts. At this point, separating fantasy from reality proved to be a most challenging ordeal. This woman, Emily Grae: How did she stop the voice of the thunder? Or did she? Was the thunder really tormenting him, or was it his imagination? Did Emily Grae really know about Jeremy? Or did he imagine that, too?

They had walked about half a mile in silence, and Michael continued his sifting of reality from fantasy. Did he imagine the part about the Seers, or were there really people who knew everything about him? Was this Emily Grae real, or had he gone completely off the deep end?

So many questions ran through his head unanswered. However, one question now surfaced above the others and caught his attention: Did he hear laughter up ahead? He was sure of it, but who, or what, was laughing? Michael was about to pose this last question to his guide, when he saw the answer he was looking for. Up ahead, running in and out of the woods, was what looked very much like a child. He appeared to be less than four feet tall, with hair of the same brilliant shade of red as Emily's. The little person was laughing loudly, and ran in and out of the woods like a child at play. Michael estimated him to be about six or seven years old, and wondered if he was perhaps Emily's son, or, more likely, a younger brother. The playful sprite stayed about fifteen feet ahead of them as they walked on.

"Miss?"

"Yes?"

"Who is that?"

"Oh, him," she said, as if he had questioned an annoying insect. "That's Hartas Glen."

"Har- *what?*" he asked.

She looked slightly annoyed, not at Michael, but at the subject of their conversation. "Hartas . . . Har-tas Glen."

"Oh." Her apparent dislike of Hartas Glen caused Michael to drop the subject. Hartas, however, had slowed down, and upon coming closer, Michael was able to hear him laughing and talking about "an Outsider coming Inside." Michael realized that he was the subject of the laughter. Hartas appeared to think that Michael coming Inside was the height of humor.

As the little one leaped and danced in and out of the woods, he stepped into the moonlight, and Michael got his first clear view of Hartas Glen. It was true, he was small, and acted like an excited child, but something didn't seem quite right. Hartas wasn't proportioned like a child. He was shaped almost like a miniature adult, and yet, even that didn't quite fit. Could Hartas be a dwarf, and not a child at all? He found himself filled with curiosity about the little anomaly. So curious, in fact, that he risked the potential displeasure of Emily Grae, and broached the subject of Hartas Glen once more.

"Miss Grae?"

"Emily. Please call me Emily."

"Emily, then. Could I ask you one more question about Hartas Glen?"

Rather than displeased, she seemed bored, but replied, "Yes, if you like."

Michael paused a moment, to frame his question inoffensively, almost as though he planned to address it to the subject himself. "How old . . . is Hartas Glen?"

Emily stopped walking for a moment, and narrowed her eyes slightly, as if trying to concentrate. "Twenty seven, I think." She, noticing Michael's surprise, continued, "You probably thought he was a child, didn't you?" He nodded. "No, he's an adult, although from the way he acts, one would never know. He stopped growing when he was six or seven. I don't really know any more about it. He insisted on being allowed to come Outside to meet you, and for some unfathomable reason, the Seers said he could." She began walking again, and Michael hurried to keep up with her.

So many questions, he thought. The Seers, this woman Emily, who knows about Jeremy, and now a twenty seven year old dwarf named Hartas Glen. It's all too much, he thought, too much.

They had now gone about a mile and a half, and Michael was exhausted. Emily, however, appeared to be in no distress. Not a hair out of place. Up ahead, there were voices. Not just Hartas laughing, but other voices. Shortly, the source came into view: An unusual sort of vehicle, with about thirteen people inside. The vehicle was open to the air, almost like a golf cart. Strangely enough, it did not have any wheels or visible means of propulsion.

As they neared the unusual vehicle, Michael noticed again the people seated in it: Men and women, all with the same red hair. The women were dressed much like Emily, in Victorian style, with similar hair fashions. The men, although they were seated, appeared tall, and were also dressed in nineteenth century attire.

Emily showed Michael a seat, and somewhat nervously, he sat next to one of the women, and directly behind a man who appeared to be the driver. Emily introduced this man as Bryan Veller. The other occupants were not introduced, but Michael clearly heard two of them expressing surprise at the appearance of an Outsider. There did not seem to be any unfriendly overtones to their comments, though, and Michael took no offense.

As he sat uncomfortably wondering whether the next stop would be Mars, Heaven, or the Twilight Zone, the sonorous boom of Bryan's voice brought him back to earth: "Hartas! Hartas Glen! If you don't get in and sit down now, you'll walk back Inside!" Some of the other passengers thought this was funny, and laughed, but Hartas wasted no time in getting in. Once inside, though, it didn't take him long to start laughing and climbing around under his seat. The others did their best to ignore him, but Michael found it somehow fascinating.

Emily sat next to Bryan, and turned to ask Michael if he was comfortable

"Yes, I'm fine. But what is this thing? Some kind of car?"

"It's called a slahm bus. It will take us Inside." She turned to face forward as the slahm began to hum. Moving forward, it began to pick up speed rapidly, going from 0 to about 120 miles per hour in less than fifteen seconds. Pinned to his seat, Michael was terrified that he would vomit. Emily turned around to look at him, and then seized Bryan by the arm. "It's too fast for him!"

Almost instantly, the slahm bus slowed to about 35 miles per hour. Turning around, Bryan said, "I'm sorry. I forgot."

With one hand on his stomach, and the other covering his mouth, Michael replied, "That's OK," hoping his green complexion wouldn't give away his condition. The other passengers seemed completely unaffected by the high-speed travel, adding to his embarrassment.

Meanwhile, under his seat, Hartas Glen was trying his best to make a spectacle of himself, mostly to no avail, since only Michael paid him any heed. Michael found himself feeling sorry for Hartas. The little man reminded him of the class misfit in St. Anselm's first grade. Michael remembered Sister Teresa trying to teach, and Thomas Jones making faces at her. Thomas didn't dislike Sister Teresa. It was just the only way he knew to get attention.

Everyone used to tease Thomas, but the first time Michael could remember feeling sorry for Thomas was on Parents' Day. All the kids had worked really hard making projects to show their visiting parents. Thomas hadn't wanted to make anything, but Sister Teresa insisted. Thomas was artistically inclined, and his project was easily the best in the class. But when Parents' Day arrived, nobody came to see Thomas' work. Sister Teresa asked him where his parents were. He started to cry, and all the kids started to laugh at him. And poor Sister Teresa, she didn't know: Thomas' father was dead, and his mother was home in a drunken stupor, her usual state. At six years of age, Thomas took care of himself. He made his own meals and walked himself to school, while his mother drank herself into oblivion. Thomas stood there crying, and finally told Sister Teresa, in front of all the kids and their parents, where his parents were. The laughing stopped. Michael had never forgotten how he felt, knowing he had laughed at Thomas. He wondered now if Hartas Glen hid some dark secret.

A splash brought Michael back to the present, as the slahm bus entered a stream about six feet wide, and, he estimated, about four feet deep. They lost no speed as they headed upstream. Michael noticed that on either side of the stream there were now concrete retaining walls, about six inches wide and rising about a foot above the water. About the same time that he noticed the walls, one of the women exhaled deeply, and said, "It sure feels good to be back Inside."

"Yes," agreed a male voice in the back, "but I won't relax completely until we're back in the Village." A few others added their assent, and Michael found himself confused. Were they Inside, or not? And what village were they talking about?

The slahm slowed to about 10 mph, and ahead of them appeared a small mountain. The stream seemed to go right into it. Upon coming closer, a tunnel entrance became visible. Michael watched in awe as the slahm bus entered the tiled passage. They traveled under the mountain for about fifty feet, and emerged in a village. There was a paved walk next to the stream, and Bryan stopped the slahm next to it.

As the passengers disembarked, they each welcomed Michael Inside, called out their good nights to each other, and began to walk away. Emily stood with Michael as Bryan started off. "I'll tell the Seers," he called over his shoulder to Emily.

"Thank you, Bryan. Give my best to Sarah when you get home." Emily turned to Michael and said, "Come on, it's late, and I know you're tired. My parents have prepared the guest room for you. In the morning, after breakfast, we'll go to the Seers. They'll answer your questions for you."

She led him through a large grassy area that appeared to be the center of the Village. As they walked, they didn't see Hartas Glen sneaking up behind them. Michael saw him just as he was about to jump in front of Emily.

"Boo!" he yelled.

Emily screamed and turned ghost-white. Hartas was laughing so hard that he fell on the ground and began to roll.

Michael was trying desperately not to laugh, not wanting to offend Emily. The whole thing got the better of him, though, and he laughed out loud.

Emily, regaining her wits, began to berate her assailant: "Hartas Glen, you creep! You scared me half to death! You're rude and inconsiderate and . . . Michael London, what are you laughing at? I certainly don't think . . ." That was as far as she got. She looked at Hartas rolling on the ground, and Michael laughing so hard he was crying, and she started to laugh, too.

Michael prodded Hartas with his foot, and said, "You'd probably better go home now, before she stops laughing. Good night, Hartas."

Still laughing, Hartas jumped to his feet and ran off. Michael offered Emily his arm, and they began to walk again. She led him to her parents' house, a large Victorian structure. In fact, as they neared the street opposite the grassy area, he noticed that nearly all the buildings looked like nineteenth century New England. And yet, anachronistically, they all seemed to have electricity. The Graes' porch light was on to welcome them.

The house was beautifully furnished. Emily's parents, Gene and Marbel Grae, were waiting up for them. According to the grandfather clock it was 11:45 p.m. The room was lit by an electric lamp, and a modern FM stereo played soft music. Mr. Grae showed Michael to the guest room, which had a private bath, and a large, comfortable bed. The furnishings were all definitely Victorian, yet appeared to be in mint condition. The plumbing fixtures, on the other hand, were completely up to date.

"Are you hungry, son?" Mr. Grae asked.

"No, sir. Well, yes, but I'm really much too tired to eat. Thank you for asking."

"Well, Mrs. Grae and I are right down the hall if you need anything. We'll call you an hour before breakfast."

"Thank you, Mr. Grae."

"Good night, Michael."

"Good night, sir." Michael took a hot shower, and collapsed into bed. He fell immediately into a deep and dreamless sleep.

5

ANOTHER TIME, ANOTHER PLACE

Michael rummaged through his suitcases for something to wear. He had been woken thirty minutes earlier by a knock, and Mrs. Grae's voice saying that breakfast would be ready in an hour, and how did he like his eggs? Now, a half hour later, he still wasn't dressed.

What was suitable? he wondered. What did one wear when presented to the Seers? Was it like church, where a suit would do? Or was it like visiting the Queen, where only very formal attire would do? As he continued to dig through his bags, there came another knock.

"Michael?"

"Mr. Grae, is that you? Come in."

"You're not dressed yet! Is something wrong?"

"Mr. Grae, I'm sorry. I really have no idea what I should wear. Emily said I'd be meeting the Seers today. What should I put on?"

The older man smiled and chuckled a little as he an-swered, "Anything you like, son. The Seers aren't ones for standing on ceremony. Just wear what makes you comfortable. I apologize:

I should have foreseen your confusion. Please forgive us: We aren't used to Outsiders, and it's difficult to remember that you don't know our ways."

Michael returned his smile, and said, "I appreciate your help. I'm kind of nervous, and I'm a little afraid of doing or saying the wrong thing. This is all so new to me. I'm still not quite used to the idea that I'm here... wherever here is."

"Don't be afraid, Michael. We who live Inside are an easy-going lot. We'll help you along. You'd better hurry now for breakfast. Emily's cooking today, and she's truly outdone herself."

The food did smell fantastic, Michael thought, as Mr. Grae closed the door. He suddenly remembered that he was very hungry. As if to speed him along, his stomach loudly growled its empty state. "Just wear what makes you comfortable," he absentmindedly said aloud, as he once again turned his attention to the piles of clothes in his suitcases. "And what makes me comfortable is a pair of jeans, and a clean shirt." He silently wished for an iron, but consoled himself by admitting that the shirt really wasn't too badly wrinkled.

He wondered if Mr. Grae really meant anything that made him comfortable. Would they consider jeans improper? He hadn't noticed any of the people wearing them last night. Maybe they didn't even know what jeans were! Well, he would certainly find out at breakfast. Emily would no doubt say something if his attire were not kosher. And speaking of kosher, he thought, or rather, non-kosher, I smell bacon! Michael, propelled by the smell of bacon and the roar of an angry stomach, quickly dressed, fixed his hair and shaved.

As he left his room, he allowed his sense of smell to guide him to the kitchen, where Mr. and Mrs. Grae were carrying food into the dining room, and Emily stood near the stove, immaculate in her floor length Victorian garb.

"Good morning, Michael," she said. "Did you sleep well?"

"Yes, thank you. Actually, I slept like a rock. I must have been really tired."

"You had a difficult day yesterday. You needed to sleep. It apparently did you a world of good: You look very well rested. Here," she said, "Would you bring these into the dining room?" She handed him a plate of hot cinnamon rolls, dripping with melted icing. As he took the plate, he dipped a finger into the icing and tasted it.

"M-m-m!" he said.

"I saw that!" she scolded in a mock-serious voice. "No samples before breakfast!"

As Michael turned toward the dining room, Mrs. Grae was coming back into the kitchen. "Good morning, Michael. You look well. Did you sleep all right?"

"Yes, ma'am, I did. Thank you." As Michael spoke to her, he noticed the strong resemblance between Mrs. Grae and her daughter. They had the same pale blue eyes: You could just look into them and see for miles. Mrs. Grae's hair had started to fade, but it still held some of the original bright red. Mr. Grae also had fading red hair, Michael noticed with amusement, but a lot less of it! So far no one had commented on his jeans, and had all had opportunity to do so.

Breakfast was delicious. He ate voraciously: Five eggs, six slices of bacon, two cinnamon rolls, six slices of toast, two glasses of orange juice, and three cups of coffee. Michael had been worried that his appetite would offend the Graes, but on the contrary, they took a parental sort of pleasure in watching him eat. Emily found it rather amusing, as judged by her smile, but said nothing.

Michael helped Mrs. Grae clear away the dishes after breakfast. As they removed the last few pieces, Mr. Grae left for work, kissing his wife and daughter, and shaking Michael's hand. Closing the door behind him, Mrs. Grae turned to Emily and said, "It's getting late, dear. Shouldn't you be off to the Hall of Seers?"

"You're right, Mother. Are you ready, Michael?"

"I guess so. Am I dressed all right?" he asked, still worried about the jeans.

"Of course," she replied. "You look fine."

Mrs. Grae smiled at Michael, and taking him by the hand, said, "Now don't you worry about anything. The Seers aren't anything to get upset about. They're good men. You can trust them." She squeezed his hand, and kissed him on the forehead, almost like a mother kissing her son and sending him off to face his first day of school. "I'll have lunch ready at noon, if you're hungry," she called out the front door as Emily and Michael left.

Seeing the Village in daylight was a shock to Michael. It was like stepping back into the 1890's. There were about twenty or so people on the streets, all in Victorian dress, and all with the same red hair. A few vehicles, similar to the slahm bus, but with room for only four or five passengers, moved down the streets.

Emily led the way across the grassy area they had crossed the night before. "This is the Village Green," she explained. "Over there is the Town Square. The tall building with the clock tower is our Town Hall. Our government is run from there, under the direction of the Seers, of course." Michael listened intently as she explained the different points of interest.

As they prepared to cross the Town Square, a large slahm, with about forty people on board, pulled up in front of the Town Hall. As the bus stopped, most of the passengers got off and went into the Town Hall or into a few other buildings nearby. Now mostly empty, the slahm moved on to its next stop.

"Public transportation?" Michael asked.

"Of course. You have buses Outside, too, don't you?" "Yes, but not without wheels. What makes them run?" "I'm sure I don't know. The Seers gave the slahms to us."

As they crossed the Town Square, Emily pointed out a two-story brick structure, painted white. "That's the Hall of Seers," she said. It was an unimpressive sight at best to Michael, who had expected a palace, or at least a Victorian mansion.

"That?"

"Yes. I know it doesn't look like much from the outside. The Seers prefer it this way. They feel it brings them closer to the people. It's also bigger than it looks. Most of the building is underground. Some say there are as many as ten floors below ground level. No one knows for sure, and the Seers aren't telling!"

Entering the front door, Michael wondered at the lack of a sign on the building, but there was no time to ask any more questions: A man in knickers and white stockings was propelling them down the hallway. Outside a large mahogany door, they paused, and Emily steered Michael toward it.

"Go ahead in," she urged.

"Aren't you coming, too?" Michael asked, suddenly panic-stricken.

"No, they want to see you alone. There's nothing to be afraid of. But it's late; they're waiting. Go in!"

Michael found himself thrust through the doorway, and into a large, dark room. At the far end, there stood a desk on a slightly raised platform. The desk area was brightly lit from an invisible source. And there, against a scarlet background, sat three men: The Seers.

6

THE SEERS

Michael stood nervously in the doorway of the room, unsure of what to do. Bow? Kneel? Salute? "The Seers aren't ones for standing on ceremony," Mr. Grae had said. But there they sat, positively god-like on their dais. As he stepped slowly into the room, he thought of The Wizard of Oz, half expecting flames to shoot out of the floor, and the Seers to bellow 'Come forward!'

The Seers were older men, about seventy five or eighty years old, Michael guessed. They wore identical purple robes, with black collars that formed a triangle on their chests.

The Seer in the middle stood as Michael approached. "Michael," he said. "Welcome. My name is Telesina. This is Harmor," he continued, indicating the Seer on his right, "and this gentleman on my left is Melfina. We are the Seers."

The three men smiled at Michael, and he began to feel slightly more at ease. Telesina motioned for Michael to come closer, and said, "No doubt you have many questions. We'll try to answer them. It was Harmor who first saw the vision that led to you being brought Inside. Perhaps he should be the one to explain."

Telesina sat as Harmor rose to his feet and walked out from behind the desk. He descended from the dais, and began to speak as he approached Michael. "It's difficult to know where to start. There is so much to tell you. Let's sit down," he said, drawing Michael to the platform and sitting on its edge. Michael sat next to him, the Seer's informal manner calming his apprehensions.

"Do you know who the Druids were, Michael?" the older man asked.

"The Druids? Not really. Didn't they live a long time ago?"

"That's right," Harmor said, "they did live a long time ago. The Druids were the religious leaders of ancient England, Ireland, Scotland and France. The French Druids died long ago, leaving no descendants. We are the descendants of the other Druids. Although we don't practice their religion, we do have their power. You might call it magic, but that isn't accurate. Our power is no more magic than your five senses. All Insiders have some of the power, but we, the Seers, have all the power of the ancient Druids, as well as the knowledge of all mankind."

"Harmor." It was Melfina who interrupted. *"Natu lehena gehelel Fortu."*

Harmor looked back at Melfina and said, "I will, I will. I can only tell him one thing at a time." Turning back to Michael, he said, "Melfina wants me to tell you about Fortu. Fortu was the secret language of the Druids in ancient times. As their descendants, all Insiders once spoke Fortu. Today, only the Seers speak it. We use it to communicate with each other and with the Seers of other Insides."

"You mean there are other places like this?" Michael interrupted.

"Oh, yes," said Harmor. "There is an Inside in Ireland, one in Scotland, and two in England. Of course, all of the Insides are completely unknown to Outsiders. You are the first Outsider ever to see an Inside. I'm sure you're wondering why you're here. I must admit I was surprised when I saw the vision of you."

"Ovu redegvu?!" Telesina exclaimed.

The Seers chuckled a little, and Harmor said, "Quite right. Melfina and Telesina were far more surprised than I was. They insisted on contacting the Seers in Ireland to see if any of them could confirm the vision. Fortunately, one of them was able to confirm. Otherwise, I think these two skeptics would have had me put away!" He laughed lightly, and then continued. "Now, the vision: I'm not at liberty to tell you everything, but I'll tell you what I can. We know about Jeremy. We'd like to extend our condolences." Telesina and Melfina murmured their assent, and Harmor went on. "After Jeremy died, you were alone. There was a very real possibility that you would become insane and suicidal. I saw in my vision that your destiny lay Inside. Therefore, I sent you a suggestion, you might say telepathically, to return home to Coalmont. I cannot tell you what your destiny will be, only that it is here, and you must find it. The Grae family has graciously offered to let you use their guest room as long as necessary. You should stay with them only until you find your destiny."

Michael stopped the Seer and asked, "Why is my destiny in here? I don't understand. Couldn't I have stayed in New York?"

"No, Michael. There was no destiny for you there."

"No destiny? What do you mean?"

Harmor looked a bit perplexed as he continued. "I'm afraid part of the problem here is the word 'destiny.' It's not actually the right word. There is no exact English equivalent for the Fortu word *'Seghva.'* With any Insider, I would simply have used the word Seghva, but I knew it would be meaningless to you, so I tried to translate it. Destiny is a poor translation.

Seghva is like a plan for a life, a future. Each person has only one Seghva. There is no English word for it because you don't have the ability to see the future as we do. Outsiders can only guess at the outcome of things. Seers, on the other hand, can know a person's Seghva. If you had remained in New York, you would have missed your Seghva. You would have..." Harmor stopped in mid-sentence. Turning to the other Seers, he asked, *"Hovan elo nato lehena?"* Both men nodded. Harmor turned back to Michael and said, "If you had stayed in New York, you would have jumped in front of a subway train."

Michael opened his mouth and tried to speak, but no words came. Harmor spoke again. "You want to know how I know: I saw you do it. But I knew as I watched that it was not your Seghva to do so. I saw your Seghva. It is here and you must find it."

Harmor stood up and walked back to his place behind the desk. "Go now, Michael. But any time you need to talk to us, we're here. Emily Grae will help you to learn our ways. You will find her an excellent teacher."

Michael stood up, and, facing the Seers, thanked them. He turned and started toward the door, still thinking about Harmor's words. Would he really have jumped in front of a train? He didn't know. He stepped out into the hallway, as the large door closed behind him of its own accord. Michael looked back at it and read the words carved into the top of the doorway: Hall of Audiences.

"Are you all right?" It was Emily. She had been speaking with the man in knickers, and had come back to the door when Michael emerged.

"Yeah, I'm OK. Those guys are something else!"

She smiled and said, "I know. I've often been surprised at the things they've told me."

Michael looked at her with curiosity. "Yeah? Like what?"

Emily smiled again. "Like when they told me you were coming Inside."

"Why did that surprise you?" he asked.

"Don't you understand, Michael? You are the first Out-sider any of us has ever seen. It was unheard of that an Outsider should come here. Why, Hildegarde Bolan practically had a stroke when she heard about it!"

"Who is Hilde- What did you say the name was? Who is that?" Michael asked.

"Hildegarde Bolan. She writes the gossip column in the newspaper. You'll get to meet her. Mrs. Bolan makes it her business to know everyone else's business. I'm surprised she hasn't cornered you already. Come on," she said, as she started toward the front door, "I'm late for work, and Mr. Taravel always gets so nervous when I'm late."

As they stepped out into the street, Emily continued. "Why don't you walk around and get to know the town. I'll meet you at home for lunch at noon." Michael nodded his assent, and Emily turned and walked about a block west, disappearing into a corner building that bore a sign identifying it as a bank.

As he watched her go, Michael stood, unsure of which way he would go. To his left, the street became a small bridge, crossing the stream. To his right, the street widened and became the Town Square. It was to the Town Square that he chose to go. There were signs at the corners, identifying the streets. The large street he was walking was called State Street. It crossed Main Street at the Square. Michael crossed State Street, entering the Village Green. On the south side of the Green was the dock area where he had arrived the night before. It was here, on the south side of the Green, that he sat on the grass, facing the dock and the stream, thinking about the words of the Seers.

7

THE FIRST DAY

"Young man!"

The imperious voice behind him caused Michael to jump quickly to his feet. Turning around, he beheld a tall woman, about sixty years of age, with her nose held aristocratically high. Her white hair was piled high in the Victorian fashion he was becoming used to. She was dressed in gray and black, and peered at him through a lorgnette.

"M-Ma'am?" Michael stuttered, awed by the queenly personage before him.

"How... do you do?" she said, with a slight trace of an upper class accent. "I am Hildegarde Bolan. I'm with the newspaper."

"Oh, the gossip column!" Michael said.

The woman's eyes widened in indignation. "Gossip column, indeed!" she replied icily. "I do not write gossip. My work appears on the same page as that of Celeste Enore." The statement was obviously meant to impress Michael, but as he'd never heard of Celeste Enore, the significance was lost.

"I beg your pardon, ma'am. I didn't mean to imply..." He stopped, not really sure of what to say.

"Well," she sniffed, "no doubt it was that Emily Grae who put that notion in your head. She'll get hers! Just wait until she reads tomorrow's column!" A wicked twinkle appeared in Hildegarde Bolan's eyes, and a slight smile appeared on her lips. Just as quickly, the smile vanished, and she addressed Michael again. "I have some questions I'd like to ask you."

"All right," he said.

"Let's sit over there," she said, indicating a bench near the stream. As they sat facing the stream, she took a small notebook from her purse and began to write with a gold colored pen. "Your name is Michael London, is it not?"

"Yes."

"You are the first Outsider ever to set foot Inside. How do you feel about this?"

"Confused," Michael responded, "very confused."

"No doubt," she said. "Now, enough trivia. I want a story! Is there any truth to the rumor that you are secretly engaged to Emily Grae?"

"What?!" Michael exclaimed. "What are you talking about?"

"I thought so," she said with a knowing look, and began to scribble furiously in her notebook. "You spent last night at the Graes' home: Is it true that Gene and Marbel Grae fight all the time? Did she threaten him with a skillet? Did he threaten to reveal dark secrets from her past?"

"Really, Mrs. Bolan, I don't know what you're talking about," said Michael, looking very bewildered.

Mrs. Bolan slapped down her pen in exasperation. "Really, Mr. London, you've got to be more cooperative," she said. "How can I write an interesting story if you won't supply me with facts?"

"Facts?" said Michael. "It sounds more like you want scandal, Mrs. Bolan. Mr. and Mrs. Grae have been very good to me. Even if the ridiculous things you said were true, I wouldn't tell you."

"Well!" she exclaimed haughtily. "This interview is over! Just wait until *you* read tomorrow's column! We'll see about scandal! Gossip column, indeed!" She stormed away, raging about "impudent Outsiders" and "that hussy, Emily Grae."

Michael watched her leave, not sure what to think. Would she really write something terrible about him? Did it matter if she did? He wondered what the Seers would say. And what if she wrote some of those things she said about the Graes? Would they think he said them?

"Hi, Michael!"

Michael turned around quickly. It was Hartas Glen. "Hartas! How are you?"

"OK. Watch me do a flip!" he said, turning somersaults on the dock pavement.

Michael turned halfway around on the bench to watch. "That's pretty good. Why don't you come sit down for a while?"

"Why?" Hartas asked, continuing his calisthenics.

"I thought we could talk for a while," Michael said.

"You want to talk to *me?*" Hartas asked, both incredulously and suspiciously. "Why?"

"Why not?" Michael countered.

Hartas stood up, and, shrugging his shoulders, walked around to the front of the bench and sat down. "What did you want to talk about?" he asked.

"I don't know," Michael said. "Why don't we talk about you?"

"Me?"

"Sure," said Michael. "Tell me about yourself."

"You mean why I'm so short, don't you?" Hartas asked, looking directly at Michael.

Michael smiled and said, "I mean *all* about you: Your family, where you live, what you like to do, you know, 'the works.'"

Hartas looked at him suspiciously again as he began, "Well, there's not much to tell. I live with my mother and my brother,

Tom. We live on Alton Street. Oh... that's across the stream, about a block over."

"Do you have a job?" Michael asked.

"Nah, who'd hire me? I just get in people's way."

"Do you have any friends?" asked Michael.

Hartas looked down at the pavement and kicked it lightly with his foot. "No," he answered in a quiet voice.

"Why not?" Michael asked. Hartas just shrugged as Michael continued. "I think you're OK, Hartas. I'd like to be your friend."

Hartas looked up at him and asked, "Don't you have any friends, Michael?"

"Well, I've got a few, but you can never have too many. Besides, I could use a friend right now: I think I just made an enemy out of Hildegarde Bolan."

Hartas wrinkled up his nose and laughed. "Oh, her!" he said. "Don't take her too seriously. Nobody does." He paused for a few seconds, and then asked, "Did you mean it when you said you wanted to be my friend?"

Michael smiled at him. "Sure," he said, and stuck out his hand. "Friends?"

"Friends!" Hartas said, and shook Michael's hand.

The two new friends sat and talked for hours. Michael told Hartas about New York, and about living Outside. He omitted any reference to Jeremy and to being gay, not sure of Hartas' views on homosexuality. Emily and the Seers knew he was gay, but he didn't know if anyone else knew.

Hartas told Michael about his father. He had died many years ago, when Hartas was only five. He told about growing up Inside, about being poor, and about being short. He also talked about being lonely, wanting so much to be noticed by anyone.

"Can I show you something, Michael?"

"Sure."

Hartas reached into his pants pocket and pulled out a small wooden statue. It was a woman, about two inches high, and carved in great detail. Every fold in her dress, every line of her hair, was carved in perfect detail.

"Hey," Michael said, "that's really something! Where'd you get it?"

"You promise not to laugh?"

"Why would I laugh? OK, I promise."

"I made it," Hartas said.

"Really?" Michael asked, "Did you really make this, Har-tas? It's beautiful!"

"Aw, it's not so good. It's just a little one. I can make bigger ones. The others are bigger," he said, showing a size of about twelve inches with his hands.

"Can I see them sometime?" Michael asked.

"Sure. I can show you this afternoon, after lunch."

Lunch! Michael thought. Looking over to the Town Hall clock, he saw that it was almost noon. Mrs. Grae would be expecting him. "Speaking of lunch, Hartas, I've got to run. Where will I meet you?" he asked.

"I can meet you here at one o'clock, OK?" Hartas said.

"Great," said Michael. "I'll see you then."

Hartas shoved the wooden figure back into his pocket and started to run toward State Street. He turned to wave, and then began to run again. Smiling, Michael waved back and walked across the Green to the Graes' house.

8

THE FIRST DAY, CONTINUED

As he crossed Main Street, Michael saw Emily coming home for lunch. He waited for her to catch up, and then asked, "How was work?"

"Boring," she said. "Taking dictation puts me to sleep. I must have done twenty-five letters this morning. But how was your morning?"

"Well," he said, as he opened the front door of the house, "I made a friend, and I made an enemy."

"An enemy? Who?" she asked, pausing in the doorway.

"Hildegarde Bolan. She..." he began.

"Ooh, wait," she interrupted, covering her mouth with her hand and giggling. "Mother has to hear this. Mother!" she called into the house. "Mother, you've got to hear this! Michael had a run-in with Mrs. Bolan!"

Mrs. Grae came into the living room, wiping her hands on a small towel. She had an amused smile on her lips as she spoke. "Mrs. Bolan? I can't wait! What did she say this time?" She propelled Michael and Emily into the dining room, where lunch was waiting.

"Well," said Michael, pouring some lemonade, "first she asked me if Emily and I were secretly engaged."

Emily began choking on her food, and then started to laugh. "Oh, that's good!" she said. "What else did she say?"

"Wait," he said, "it gets better."

"I can hardly wait," said Mrs. Grae with obvious enthusiasm.

"OK, are you ready for this?" Michael asked. "She asked me if Mr. and Mrs. Grae fight all the time, and if ... Wait, let me see if I can do this like her." Michael took his knife and napkin, and holding them like pen and notebook, adopted Hildegarde Bolan's posture and accent. "Did she threaten him with a skillet?" he mimicked, as Emily and her mother convulsed with laughter. He continued, "Did he threaten to reveal dark secrets from her past?"

"Oh, please, stop!" Mrs. Grae sputtered as she laughed. "I can't catch my breath!"

"That's about all there was," he said. "I accused her of wanting a scandal, and she got all bent out of shape. She implied that she was going to write something terrible about me tomorrow."

"Of course," said Emily. "Why should *you* be any differ-ent? There's hardly a person alive she hasn't done that to. Except the Seers, of course."

"Then I shouldn't worry about it?" he asked.

"Worry?" asked Mrs. Grae. "Of course not. Nobody believes what she writes."

"You mean nobody reads her column?" Michael asked.

Emily laughed as her mother answered, *"Everybody* reads her column. Nobody *believes* it."

"Then why do they read it?" he asked.

"Because it's funny," Emily said. "Mrs. Bolan is the only one who thinks her column is serious."

"Well, that's a relief," Michael said. "I'm almost looking forward to reading it."

"Enough about Mrs. Bolan, already," Emily said. "You said you made a friend. Who is it?"

Michael hesitated before answering. He knew Emily wasn't overly fond of Hartas Glen. Would she disapprove?

"Well?" she asked again. "Who is it?"

"It's Hartas Glen," he said.

"Hartas Glen?!" she asked incredulously. "Are you serious?"

"Yes, I'm serious. I spent half the morning talking with him. And from what he tells me, that's something not many people Inside have ever taken the time to do. He's a really nice guy."

"Well," she said doubtfully, "if you say so."

"I do say so, Emily," Michael said. "Give him a chance. He's intelligent, talented and sensitive. He's also very lonely." Emily did not respond. Mrs. Grae smiled at him, but she, too, said nothing.

After lunch, Emily left to return to work. It was only twenty minutes to one, so Michael stayed and helped Mrs. Grae with the dishes. "Emily isn't very happy with my choice of friends, is she?" he asked.

"No, she isn't," Mrs. Grae said. "But it isn't so much because she dislikes Hartas. I'm not sure if I can explain this; it's kind of, well, embarrassing. You see, our family is fairly well off. All of our neighbors are well-to-do. Emily grew up with the elite of Inside. Hartas Glen is from a very poor family. I'm afraid Emily's attitude is our fault. We never actually taught her to look down on poorer families, but we also never taught her *not* to. Emily has some very important lessons to learn. So don't give up on Hartas, Michael. You may be the friend he so very much needs, and you might just help my daughter to learn something, too."

Michael crossed the Village Green toward the dock and saw Hartas waiting for him. "You're early!" he shouted as he approached.

Hartas laughed. "Do you still want to see the things I've carved?" he asked.

"You bet I do. Where are they?" Michael asked.

"At my house. I wanted you to meet my Mom, too," Hartas said. "OK?"

"Sure, I'd love to."

They walked along the edge of the Green toward State Street. There was a small street called Center Lane, which connected the dock with State Street. There was only one building on Center Lane. It housed two stores, one, a book-store, and the other, vacant. The stream ran directly behind the building.

When they reached State Street, they turned right, crossing a bridge over the stream. The next right hand turn was Alton Street. The Glens' house was the second building on the left side of Alton, next to a grocery store. A one-story frame building, the house desperately needed paint.

Hartas led the way onto the porch and pushed the door open. "Mom?" he called out. Michael stepped into the room behind Hartas. It was dark, except for a floor lamp. Mrs. Glen sat in a worn armchair next to the lamp, sewing. "Mom," said Hartas, "This is my friend, Michael London. Michael, this is my mother, Arla Glen."

Mrs. Glen put down her sewing and rose to her feet. Her hair was white, and hung freely down her back. She wore a plain, brown skirt, floor length, and a white blouse. "Michael," she said, putting out both her hands and taking his, "I'm so pleased to meet you. It's true; you really do have dark brown hair! How extraordinary!"

"Mrs. Glen, I'm honored," Michael said.

"Please sit down," she said, indicating a threadbare sofa with several patches. "Hartas, be a dear, and fetch your friend some refreshment." As Hartas disappeared from the room, Mrs. Glen leaned forward from her chair and whispered to Michael, "My son has never had a friend. He's a very lonely man, and easily hurt. Forgive me," she continued, "but I must ask: Are you really his friend? You weren't just teasing him, were you?"

"No, Mrs. Glen. Please believe me: I think Hartas is a really nice person. I'm proud to be his friend. I mean that."

"Thank you, Michael," she said. "I'm sorry that I had to ask, but Hartas has had so much pain in his life, I wanted to protect him. Forgive me."

"I understand, Mrs. Glen. You can trust me. I won't hurt him."

Hartas reentered with a pitcher of lemonade and three glasses. They sat and made small talk for a while, and then Hartas asked Michael to come see his carvings.

"These are incredible!" Michael said. He stood in the bedroom that Hartas and Tom shared, and looked at the hundred or so wooden statues that lined the walls. Every available spot held a figure. Most were about a foot in height, and carved in great detail. There were carvings of men, women, children, animals and buildings. There was even a model of the Town Hall, perfect in every detail, from the tower on the roof, down to the movable hands on the clock.

"How long does something like this take to carve?" Michael asked, picking up the figure of a woman.

"About a day and a half, I guess. Do you like them?" Hartas asked.

"Very much," Michael said. Looking more carefully at the figure in his hand, he realized that it looked familiar. Suddenly, he burst out laughing. "Why, it's Hildegarde Bolan!"

"Yeah," said Hartas. "She even has those silly glasses she holds up to her face. They were hard to carve."

Holding Mrs. Bolan in his hand, Michael said, "Hartas, I have an idea. Can I borrow one of these?"

"Sure, but what for?"

"I'd rather not say just yet. I've got to talk to some people first. Then I'll let you know, I promise." Hartas shrugged his shoulders and nodded.

Voices from outside the room now caught their attention. Turning to the doorway, they saw a tall young man accompanied by a young woman. "Hi," Hartas said to the two. "I'd like you to meet my friend, Michael London. Michael, this is my brother Tom, and his girlfriend, Barbara Seal."

Michael shook hands with the couple.

Barbara giggled a little, and said, "Excuse me. I'm a little nervous. I've never met an Outsider before."

"So who has?" Tom kidded her.

"It's nice to meet you, Michael," he continued. "Has my brother been showing you his hobby?"

"Yes. He's pretty talented, isn't he?"

"I guess he is," Tom said. "Well, we've really got to go. We've got a bunch of errands to run, and Barb's parents expect us for dinner in a few hours. It was nice to meet you."

9

WELCOME TO HIGH SOCIETY

Entering the kitchen, Gene Grae leaned against the refrigerator door and addressed his wife, who was kneeling in the pantry, rearranging items on the bottom shelf.

"Marbel, do you have a moment?"

"What is it, dear?" she asked, not looking up.

"I just sent Michael down the block to rent a dinner jacket," her husband said.

"Why?" she asked, half turning to look at him.

"An invitation. Mrs. Enore's maid, Regina, just called. There's a formal dinner party tonight in Michael's honor."

Mrs. Grae stopped her pantry organizing, and said, "I do wish Celeste Enore would learn the concept of advance notice. Does she really think the whole world can stop and start at her command? We should decline."

"Be realistic, my dear. We can't decline: The party is for Michael. Besides, consider the social implications: Nobody refuses Celeste Enore. It simply isn't done."

"I suppose you're right. Anyway, I can wear my new gown. Mrs. Enore will simply drop dead from envy when she sees it. I can hardly wait!"

Michael appeared in the doorway. "Excuse me," he said. "Michael," Mr. Grae said, "Come in. Do you know who Celeste Enore is?"

"I've heard the name," Michael said, "but I don't know who she is."

"Mrs. Enore writes the Society Column for the paper. In matters of elitism, her word is law. You might say she *is* Society. Mrs. Enore is hosting a formal dinner party at her home tonight to honor you. All of Inside society will be there. It will give you a chance to meet more people. By the way, Mrs. Bolan will be there, too. She and Mrs. Enore are best friends. Mrs. Bolan will probably pretend that she is meeting you for the first time. It's some kind of ritual that only she understands. Just play along with it."

"Oy, vey," Michael groaned, rolling his eyes.

"Oy, vey?" echoed Mr. and Mrs. Grae, exchanging uncomprehending looks.

At 7:30 p.m., Mr. and Mrs. Grae, Emily and Michael stood outside Mrs. Enore's house, which was next door to their own. The door was answered by a young woman wearing a black and white maid's uniform, a stark contrast to her red hair.

"Good evening, Regina." said Mrs. Grae. "This is Mr. London."

The young woman curtseyed. "Good evening, sir. I'm pleased to meet you." She took their coats, and led them to the doorway of a large room filled with immaculately dressed men and women. Standing in the doorway, she announced in a loud, clear voice, "Gene and Marbel Grae, Ms. Emily Grae of Main Street. The guest of honor, Mr. Michael London of Outside." She curtseyed and withdrew, leaving Michael and the Graes in the doorway.

At Regina's mention of Michael's name, the assembled guests burst into spontaneous applause, and rushed forward, eager to meet him. Michael was backed against a wall, swamped by a sea of hands and voices: "I'm Dr. Whitstone." "I'm Mrs. Tey." "I'm Martin Taravel." Completely overwhelmed, Michael just stared at the crowd.

One voice, a woman's voice, now rose above the others. "Make way, make way! Back, you vultures! Give him air! Make way!" Obediently, the mass of people backed away and parted for the owner of the voice. A heavyset woman in her mid-sixties, with white hair strikingly coiffed, made her way through the press. Her gown was off-white and covered with pearls and lace. On her bosom she wore a cameo brooch. Proffering her hand to be kissed, she spoke, "I am Celeste Enore. Please forgive the poor manners of this mob. They don't know how to behave properly."

Michael bowed slightly to kiss her hand. "I'm pleased to meet you, Mrs. Enore. I've heard so much about you."

"I have no doubt," she replied. "Let me introduce you." Mrs. Enore took him by the hand and led him around the room, introducing the approximately seventy-five people assembled. Just as Mr. Grae had predicted, Mrs. Bolan gave no indication that she and Michael had met previously. When Mrs. Enore introduced her, she peered at him through her lorgnette, and extended her hand. Michael concealed his amusement as he thought of Hartas' statue of Mrs. Bolan, and her "silly glasses."

Finally left to mingle on his own, Michael found Emily talking with a young man about her own age. "Michael," she said, "this is Alan Okun, a very good friend of mine. Alan, this is Michael London."

The two shook hands, and Alan said, "Emily and I were wondering if you would join us for a slahm ride on Saturday afternoon. Emily is making a picnic lunch."

"That sounds like fun!"

"Good. I'll pick you both up at noon." To Emily, he added pointedly, "You be ready!"

Emily feigned surprise and said, "Why, Alan Okun, when have I ever been late?"

"Today," he began, "yesterday, the day before, the day before that."

"Stop that!" she said. "I'll be ready at noon." To Michael, she added, "He always teases me about being late."

The party couldn't end soon enough for Michael. He felt like a museum piece on public display. All through dinner, they seemed to stare at him, as though he might eat strangely because he was from Outside. When the festivities ended, Emily and Alan went for a walk on the Green, and Michael accompanied the Graes home.

"So tell me," Mr. Grae said, sitting on the edge of Michael's bed, "What did you think of Mrs. Enore and the 'upper crust' of Inside?"

"Well, Mrs. Enore was OK, but I don't remember half of the people she introduced me to."

"Don't worry. You'll get to know them. My wife tells me you made a friend today."

"Uh, yes. Hartas Glen."

"That's good," said Mr. Grae. "He needs a friend. And don't worry about Emily's less than enthusiastic reaction. She'll come around in time. She just has a little growing up to do."

"Mr. Grae, can I show you something?"

"Sure, son. What is it?"

Michael opened one of the bureau drawers and withdrew the wooden figure of Hildegarde Bolan. He handed it to Mr. Grae and waited.

"It's Hildegarde Bolan!" the man exclaimed. "Where did you get it? Look at the detail!"

"Before I tell you where it came from, tell me honestly what you think it's worth," Michael said.

"Oh, something this beautiful couldn't go for less than fifty Sheryls," he said, still admiring the craftsmanship. Noting Michael's blank expression, he added, "Oh, Sheryls... I forgot. Let me see if I can remember. I think a Sheryl is about one and a half of your dollars, but don't quote me."

"Then it's valuable?" Michael asked.

"Oh, certainly. But now, out with it: Where did you get it?" Mr. Grae asked.

"I'd like you to promise not to say anything to anyone, OK?" Michael said.

"Well, if you insist. I promise. Now please, where did it come from?"

Michael smiled cryptically as he answered, "This piece was handcrafted by a very talented artist. It took him less than two days to produce this magnificent figurine."

Mr. Grae's impatience grew. "Who, already? Who?" "Hartas," Michael said, still smiling.

"Hartas?! Hartas Glen? He made this?" Mr. Grae asked incredulously.

"This," Michael said, "and dozens more. There's more to Hartas Glen than meets the eye!"

"Oy, vey!" said Mr. Grae, and they both laughed.

10

FRIDAY

In the morning, after Emily and her father had left for work, Michael asked Mrs. Grae, "Would you show me how to use the telephone?"

"Certainly. It's quite simple, really, and I'm told that our system is similar to Outside, so you shouldn't have any trouble." There was a phone on a small end table in the living room, and Mrs. Grae held it up. It was a rather ordinary, brown plastic pushbutton phone. "All homes and businesses have telephones like this. Our phones are free. I understand that Outsiders must pay for phone service."

"Yes, we pay... dearly!"

"Now, of course," she went on, "we can't call Outside, and Outside can't call in. To make a call, you just push the four-digit number. There's a directory in the drawer, and everyone's number is in it. In an emergency, you call the Operator at Telephone Central. You just push "0" for Operator. Our number is 6047." She pressed the buttons as she spoke, and held the phone to Michael's ear.

"Busy signal," he said. "Just like Outside."

While Mrs. Grae was in the kitchen cleaning up the aftermath of breakfast, Michael sat in the living room reading the telephone directory. The listings took only two pages. He found the listing Hall of Seers, followed by the instructions *In an emergency, push 0. For information, appointments, etc., push 5555. If busy, 3333.*

Michael picked up the phone and pressed 5555. It rang once, and a woman answered. "Hall of Seers. May I have your name, please?"

"Michael London.

"Good morning, Mr. London. Welcome Inside. What may I do for you?"

"I'd like an appointment with the Seers, please."

"One moment, please," she said, putting him on hold. "Mr. London? Monday morning at nine is your appointment."

"I had hoped for something today," he said.

"I'm sorry," she said. "Please understand that the Seers know the situation, and they feel that Monday is best."

"All right. Monday at nine. Thank you." Michael hung up the phone and looked up another listing: Glen, Mrs. Arla, Alton St. - 1624. He picked up the phone and dialed. Hartas answered on the third ring.

"Hello?"

"Hartas?"

"Yeah?"

"Hi, it's Michael. How are you doing?"

"Fine," he said. "How about you?"

"Great. Listen, what's on your agenda for today?" Michael asked.

"Nothing. Why?" Hartas asked. "You got any suggestions?"

"No," Michael said, "but as long as we're both doing nothing, why don't we do it together?"

"Sounds good to me," Hartas said. "How about the dock in fifteen minutes?"

"You got it," Michael said "See you there."

"Are you going to tell me now?" Hartas asked Michael when they met on the dock.

"Tell you what?" Michael asked.

"The mysterious plan you wouldn't tell me about yesterday."

"I can't tell you yet; it's too soon. I'll tell you all about it Monday afternoon or evening," Michael promised. "I'll give you back your statue of Mrs. Bolan then, too. In the meantime, she's safe in my room at the Graes' house."

Hartas smiled crookedly, and said, "You know, of course, that I'm dying of curiosity."

"Curiosity killed the cat," Michael countered with a grin.

"Cat?" Hartas said, with a puzzled look. "What cat?"

Laughing, Michael slapped him on the back. "Never mind," he said. "It's just a figure of speech."

The two spent the day exploring the town, with Hartas pointing out the places of interest. From the dock, they headed north toward State Street via Center Lane, passing the bookstore and the empty store. Turning left on State Street, they stood in the Town Square, with the Town Hall on their right, and the Village Green on their left. Here, Main Street crossed State. Across Main, the Graes' house was on the left corner, the bank on the right.

"Let's go up Main Street," Hartas suggested. They turned right on Main, putting the bank on their left, and the Town Hall on their right. As they walked north on Main, Hartas pointed out the newspaper offices next to the bank, and, across the street, attached to the Town Hall, the Town Office Building. Next door to the newspaper was a plain brick building, which Hartas identified as Telephone Central. On the other side of this structure, West Alexander Avenue crossed Main Street. Across Main was a large, brick mansion. "This," said Hartas, with an aristocratic accent, "is the home of Hildegarde Bolan.

Please pass with awe." His friend's near perfect imitation of the columnist convulsed Michael with laughter.

Turning right, Michael noticed by the street signs that east of Main Street, West Alexander Avenue was just Alexander Avenue. Across Alexander from Mrs. Bolan's house was a large, modern brick building. Seeing Michael's interest, Hartas offered, "The auditorium. The rich people hold a lot of their parties there, and most holiday celebrations are held there."

As they continued east on Alexander Avenue, they passed a glass and aluminum structure, next door to Mrs. Bolan's house. It had a sign in front saying Tolfesor Elementary School. "Tolfesor?" Michael questioned.

"Tolfesor. She was a Seer when the first elementary school was built here," Hartas explained.

"She?" asked Michael. "There are women who are Seers, too?"

"Of course," Hartas said. "Telesina became Seer when his mother, Wandela died. She had been Seer for sixty-two years. Right now, all our Seers here are men, but there are three female Seers in Europe. We'll have some again when Melfina and Telesina die. They both have daughters who are future Seers. Harmor's successor will be his son, Thomas. A Seer's oldest child inherits the position. If the Seer has no children, he or she appoints a successor from among the children of the other Seers, or from among his or her own younger siblings."

As Hartas finished his explanation, they crossed a bridge over the stream. On the other side, Michael's attention was taken by a huge, metal structure on the left side of Alexander Avenue. From the large doors across the front, Michael took it to be a garage of some kind.

"Slahm buses," said Hartas, perceiving the question. "They're kept here at night."

Across the street, another aluminum and glass building stood. Its sign said Sinevor-Tesha High School. "Let me guess," said Michael. "Two old Seers?"

"Close," said Hartas. "One old Seer and his wife. The school was her idea." Just past the school, a short street headed south from Alexander Avenue. The sign identified it as North Alton Street. Across from the school on this street was a small diner. Michael and Hartas turned onto North Alton. The high school took up the entire block to their right, while the diner and a small house were the only structures on their left.

North Alton Street ended at Timothy Drive, where they turned right. The back of the high school was on their right, and a hardware store on their left. Beyond the school, Timothy Drive ended at the stream, and School Road headed south. Turning left onto it, they passed a small shed, attached to the rear of the hardware store. Through the window of the shed, they could see a tailor working at his sewing machine. The hardware store and the tailor's shed were the only buildings on School Road.

Past the tailor, School Road ended at East State Street. A candy store stood opposite School Road. Turning left, they walked a short distance east, to the place where Alton Street intersected East State Street, heading south. "Hey," said Michael, "I know where we are: This is your street!"

"Right," said Hartas. On the east side of Alton Street was a grocery store, next to which stood the Glens' house. Across from the dilapidated house stood a barbershop, and just south of the house was a brick structure with a tall metal tower behind it. The sign over the building's entrance said Radio Inside.

Sitting on the Glens' front porch, Michael and Hartas spent the remainder of the morning talking. Hartas talked about his years in school, being the "class clown." He talked about rejection and being alone. Michael listened quietly to the things his friend said. What he said about being alone struck a chord in Michael. He thought of Jeremy. He thought of his parents. He thought of Laura.

"Tell me about your father, Hartas.

"Well, like I told you yesterday, he died when I was five."

"Do you remember him at all?"

Hartas paused before he spoke. In his eyes, a faraway kind of look appeared. He smiled slightly. "Yes. He was tall. He looked a lot like Tom. He used to come home from work and call out 'Where are my boys?' Tom and me, we'd come running out of the house, and he'd pick us up and say..." He stopped, and Michael saw that he was crying.

"Hartas, you don't have to..."

"No," Hartas interrupted, wiping his tears. "It's OK. He'd say 'Who does Daddy love?' And we'd both shout 'Me!' He'd say 'Right!' and then he'd hug us both and put us down. I cried for weeks when he died."

"My parents both died a few years ago," Michael said. "Their house caught fire, and they were trapped inside. I had nightmares about it for a long time. What did your father do for a living?"

Hartas didn't answer right away. He looked away for a moment, and then said, "He was a sanitation worker."

Michael laughed out loud. "A garbage man?! So was mine!"

"You're kidding! Was he really?" They laughed till tears came.

When it came time for lunch, Michael headed back to the Graes' house. As he mounted the porch steps, Emily flew out the front door. "Where have you been?" she screamed hysterically. "You're five whole minutes late! Have you seen this yet? You'll just die!" she raved, waving a newspaper wildly in the air.

Bewildered, Michael let her drag him into the living room. "There," she said, shoving him into a chair. "Sit there. Now, read this!" she commanded, thrusting the paper into his hands. "Well?" she demanded.

"Well," he said calmly, "it's upside down."

Exasperated, she snatched the paper away and presented it again in a more readable direction. As Emily bounced off the walls with anticipation, Michael read the cause of her agitation. The headlines read 'Drunken Outsider Creates Scene as Pregnant Daughter Causes Graes' Divorce.' Again he read the headlines. And again.

At that moment, Mrs. Grae entered the room. Emily snatched the paper back from Michael, and said, "You read too slow. Let me read it to you. Mother, sit down." Compelling the woman to sit, Emily cleared her throat and read the headlines aloud.

"Oh," said Mrs. Grae, laughing, "Mrs. Bolan's column! This ought to be good."

Emily held up her hand to regain the floor, and continued. "A shocking display of wanton drunkenness took place last night at the home of Mrs. Celeste Enore on Main Street. The inebriated guest was none other than Mr. Michael London, our by now infamous Outsider. Such behavior, we are told, is common among Outsiders. We can only guess at the embarrassment of the much put-upon hostess, Mrs. Enore, as the drunken Mr. London careened across the room, brazenly propositioning members of some of Inside's best families with lewd suggestions. Said Mrs. Sandra Tey, wife of Vicar Marcus Chelwith, 'I'm just aghast . . . I'm speechless!' And Mrs. Alora Cern Whitstone, who incidentally, is still recovering from the sensational divorce scandal of last summer (check your back issues, folks!), said, 'I can't imagine how such a thing could happen. Someone should have done something.' Meanwhile, Ms. Emily Grae, also of Main Street, was creating a sensation of her own, announcing to the entire assemblage that she is with child. Rumor has it that Mr. Bryan Veller of Lost Acre Road is the father.

His wife, Mrs. Sarah Veller, poor dear, has reportedly asked the Seers for permission to divorce the cad and to emigrate to a European Inside. The reaction of Ms. Grae's distraught parents was understandable, considering the poor state of relations in their own crumbling marriage. Mr. Gene Grae reportedly began to accuse Mrs. Marbel Grae, his wife of twenty-nine years, of infidelity. She, in turn, physically attacked him in plain sight of the shocked onlookers. Asked for her views on the spectacle that took place in her home, Mrs. Celeste Enore replied, 'I shall never be the same again.' That's all for today, dear Readers. We'll be back again tomorrow with more interesting news, and perhaps an update on the scandal involving our dear pastor Vicar Marcus Chelwith, and his alleged mistress, ninety two year old widow Ms. Letitia Cern Shea."

As Emily finished reading, Michael sat in shocked silence, his mouth open. "Isn't that too much?" Emily squealed.

With a certain amount of awe in her voice, Mrs. Grae responded, "Well, Mrs. Bolan has certainly outdone herself. She got all of us, the Whitstones, the Vicar and his wife, the Vellers and Ms. Shea, all in one column. I'll bet that's a new record."

"Well?!" Emily demanded, looking at Michael and stamping her foot. "What do you think?"

"Oh, my God," he said. "Oh, my God."

"Michael," Mrs. Grae said, reaching out and taking his hand. "Remember, it's all in fun. Nobody believes a word of it. Trust me."

Nodding, Michael responded, "Oh, my God."

More than amused by his reaction, Emily began to tease him about propositioning the Vicar's wife. When he had relaxed enough to think clearly, he, too, began to laugh. As the three sat laughing and trading quotes from the article, the phone rang. Mrs. Grae answered it, while Emily and Michael continued to laugh at Mrs. Bolan's outrageous story.

"It's for you, Michael," said Mrs. Grae, handing him the phone. "It's the Vicar's wife," she added in a whisper.

Instantly serious, Michael took the phone, fearing what the minister's wife would say. Would she be angry? Insulted? "Hello?" he whispered into the phone.

"Michael?" asked the voice on the line. "This is Sandra Tey, Vicar Chelwith's wife. We met last night at Mrs. Enore's."

"Yes, ma'am. How are you?"

"I'm just fine, thank you. I'm calling about Mrs. Bolan's column. I suppose you've seen it?"

"Yes, ma'am. We just read it."

"Quite a hatchet job, wasn't it? I was just afraid that nobody had warned you . . . No one believes what Mrs. Bolan writes."

"Yes, that's what I've been told. I'm sure glad!"

"So am I!" she said with a chuckle. "I was just worried about you, and thought I'd call to reassure you."

"I do appreciate it, Mrs. . . . uh . . ." he fumbled, unsure of how to address her.

"Mrs. Tey," she said, supplying the needed information. "Tey is my own name. The spouses of Vicars and Seers always keep their own family name."

"Mrs. Tey," he repeated. "Thank you very much. I appreciate your concern."

"Well," she said, "if you need anything, give us a call. Will we see you in church on Sunday?"

"Yes, ma'am. I'll be there."

11

WEEKEND

On Saturday morning, Michael and the Graes slept late, not rising until after ten o'clock. The Graes ate a quick brunch, but Michael, not feeling hungry, decided to call Hartas.

Mrs. Glen answered the phone. "I'm sorry, Michael. Hartas isn't home. He'll be busy all day. He and Tom are doing some yard work over at the high school. He asked me to tell you that he'll see you tomorrow."

Michael thanked her and hung up. It was nearly eleven; Alan would be by in an hour to pick them up for the slahm ride. Entering the dining room, he asked Emily, "Have you made lunch for this afternoon?"

"Why, Michael," she replied, "what a question! Do you really think I'm as unprepared as that? One would think I was the type to put things off until the last minute! I mean, really!"

"I'm sorry." he apologized. "I was just asking."

"Asking what?" she questioned innocently.

"If you'd made lunch yet."

"No, I didn't," she said, exiting hastily into the kitchen, giggling.

"My daughter," Mr. Grae said, smiling at his wife and Michael, "a paragon of intelligence!" Under his breath, he added, "I.Q. of a raisin!"

"From her *father's* side of the family," said Mrs. Grae with a quick smile, as she, too, made a dash for the kitchen. Michael and Mr. Grae looked at each other and shared a good laugh.

Mr. Grae motioned for Michael to join him at the table. As Michael sat, Mr. Grae said to him, "So tell me: What kind of scheme are you cooking up?"

"Sir?" Michael asked, not understanding.

"Those statues Hartas Glen makes," Mr. Grae said. "You're working on some kind of plan, aren't you?"

"Well, yes, but it's just an idea. I won't have anything definite until I talk with the Seers. I have an appointment with them Monday morning." The older man seemed satisfied, and asked no further questions.

The doorbell rang as Michael helped Mr. Grae clear the dishes. "Oh, my God!" Emily screamed from the kitchen. "I'm not ready!" She raced into the living room and up the stairs, two at a time, to her room.

"I don't think that's Alan," said her mother, coming out of the kitchen to answer the door. "It's too early." She opened the door to a very thin, frail old woman. The woman wore a blue housedress, carried a cane, and had her white hair piled haphazardly on her head. "Why, Ms. Shea!" exclaimed Mrs. Grae. "Please come in. What a pleasant surprise!"

"Yes!" agreed the old woman with a delighted, toothless grin. She hobbled in, and, seeing Michael, squinted, as if to see better. Raising her eyebrows, she then fixed one eye upon him, closing the other. She lifted her cane, as if to strike him, and whispered to Mrs. Grae, "Is he from Mars?"

"No, Ms. Shea," she answered quickly, gently lowering the woman's cane. "He's not from Mars. This is Michael London, from Outside." The old woman again stared at him from one eye. "Michael," Mrs. Grae continued, "this is Letitia Cern Shea. Ms. Shea lives around the corner on State Street with her niece, Mrs. Whitstone." Standing behind Ms. Shea, Mrs. Grae tapped her own forehead with her index finger, to signal to Michael that the old woman had a "problem." Catching the signal, he nodded slightly, smiled, and extended his hand to Ms. Shea. Raising her cane menacingly, the old woman backed up into Mrs. Grae.

"Don't you come near me!" she warned. "Are you sure he's not from Mars, Marbel?" she asked. "He looks mighty peculiar to me."

"I'm very sure, Ms. Shea. He's from Outside."

"Hmph!" the old woman said, unconvinced. Eyeing him suspiciously, she made her way to the sofa, careful to give Michael a wide berth. "There was a rainbow in my coffee this morning," said Ms. Shea as she sat down. "That always means I'll see a Martian," she asserted, carefully watching Michael, in case he began to sprout antennae.

"Well, that's interesting, Ms. Shea," said Mrs. Grae. "Would you like some tea?" she added, hoping to change the topic of conversation.

"Yes, thank you," the old woman replied, adding quickly, "Make sure it's tea, not coffee! Coffee has rainbows! Have you ever tasted a rainbow?" she asked, directing her question to Michael.

"No, ma'am," he answered, shaking his head.

"No, I don't suppose you have," she said. "They probably don't have rainbows on Mars. Well, let me tell you, they're terrible. Oh, they look pretty enough, but the taste... They taste like earwax!"

"Oh," said Michael, wondering how she knew what earwax tasted like. The thought made him feel somewhat queasy. For the next twenty minutes, he sat in awe, listening to Ms. Shea rambling on about cats in her bathtub, Martian spies in her linen closet, friendly elves in her sugar bowl, and invisible butterflies that were trying to steal her cup of tea. Mr. and Mrs. Grae listened politely, occasionally interrupting to clarify certain details: What color cats? How many elves? And did she want a fly swatter to chase the butterflies?

At three minutes to twelve, the doorbell rang again. From upstairs came a shriek: "Tell him I'm almost ready!"

Mr. Grae opened the door to admit Alan. Ms. Shea, looking up, asked Mrs. Grae, "Then is *that* the Martian?"

Alan took a seat, and Michael whispered to him, "Emily's almost ready."

"Ha!" Alan said. "Don't count on it: She'll be at least another twenty minutes, or I don't know Emily Grae!" Turning their attention to Ms. Shea, now defending her third cup of tea from the malevolent butterflies, they listened.

"So what could I do?" the old woman was saying. "I couldn't let all of Inside be swept away just like that. A whole army of Martians with giant brooms! But I know a secret: I know how to get rid of Martians. Do you know what it is?" No one did. "Parsley!" she exclaimed triumphantly. "Everyone should know that: It's common knowledge. Martians can't tolerate parsley. So I took some parsley from my kitchen, and I went out to the Town Square. I threw it up into the air: One, two, three, twenty handfuls of parsley! The wind carried it all over, and it killed those Martians." Turning to Mrs. Grae, she whispered behind her hand, "Just between you and me, Marbel, I'd throw some parsley on those two," indicating Michael and Alan. "They look like Martians to me." Mrs. Grae said that she would certainly give the suggestion some thought, winking at the accused extraterrestrials.

It was almost twelve thirty when Emily came downstairs. Taking the hastily prepared lunch, she called out, "Bye! Goodbye, Ms. Shea!" To Michael and Alan, she added, "Come on."

Waving goodbye, they left Gene and Marbel Grae to their fate of spending the afternoon with Ms. Letitia Cern Shea. As the two men followed Emily out the door, Ms. Shea was already engrossed in relating a story about pixies that had stolen her dentures, and she couldn't find the teeth for a week. Apparently, the mischievous sprites had hidden them from her... in a glass of water on her nightstand.

Outside the house, Alan asked Michael, "Was that your first time meeting Ms. Shea?"

"Yeah. What's the story?"

"Well, she's harmless. She's gotten a little senile over the years. Sometimes she can be really funny to listen to. There's actually more to the story about why she is the way she is. I'd only get it all wrong if I tried to tell it. Why not ask the Seers about her?" he suggested. "They could explain it much better."

12

PICNIC

Parked outside the Graes' house was a smaller version of the slahm that had first brought Michael Inside. There was room enough for the driver and three passengers. Emily and Alan sat in front, and Michael climbed into the back.

"Where are we going?" Michael asked, as Alan started the slahm.

"Surday Park," Emily answered, turning around in her seat, "It's near the northern edge of Inside."

"Surday?" Michael asked, "Was that the name of a Seer?"

"Yes," said Emily, "The park was named after her about a hundred and fifty years ago. She was very popular. There's a book about her at the library, if you're interested."

"It does sound interesting. You'll have to show me where the library is."

Emily nodded in assent. The slahm was heading north on Main Street, passing the newspaper office, Telephone Central, and Hildegarde Bolan's house. They continued north, crossing Alexander Avenue and passing the auditorium. Michael estimated their speed at about 15 or 20 mph, but as they passed the auditorium, Alan accelerated to about 60.

"What's the top speed for an Outsider, Emily?" he asked.

"The Seers said to keep it to about 50," she responded, "They can tolerate more, but they advised against it."

As Alan slowed to fifty, Emily turned again to Michael. "Is 50 miles an hour comfortable for you, Michael?"

"Oh, yeah," he said, "It's fine. But how fast do you usually go?"

"Outside the village, we usually do about 150," Alan volunteered, "Inside the village, never more than 20."

"But how can you stand such high speeds?" Michael asked, "Don't you get sick?"

"No," Alan said, "It doesn't affect us. Have the Seers explained to you that we're descended from the Druids?"

"Yes," Michael said.

"Well, that's why things affect us differently," Alan explained, "To put it in more scientific terms, we're a different species."

"A different species!?" Michael exclaimed, "What do you mean? Aren't you human?"

"Well, yes and no," Alan said.

"Oh, *that's* a good answer!" teased Emily.

"What I mean is this," he continued. "You belong to the species *Homo Sapiens,* right?"

"Yes," Michael agreed.

"Well, we're not *Homo Sapiens.* We share the same genus, that is, *Homo,* but the species is different. We belong to the species *Homo Mirabilis.* That's why we're different."

"Oh," said Michael, "Are there any other differences?"

"There are lots," said Emily, "For example, all Insiders have red hair, blue eyes and light skin. Outsiders have much more variety. We're told that Outsiders have four basic skin colors, with some shades in between. Is that true?"

"Yeah," Michael said, "Basically, we come in black, white, red and yellow. And we have all kinds of eye colors, like black, brown, blue, hazel, green. Mine are hazel, but sometimes they change to green or gray."

"That's fascinating," Emily said, turning to look at Michael's eyes, "They look green now. It must be great to have so much variety."

"I guess so," he said, "But tell me more about Insiders."

"All Insiders have certain abilities," Alan began, "For example, we can temporarily reduce our body weight by more than two-thirds."

"Huh?" Michael said, "What do you mean?"

"I can explain," Emily interjected, "Do you remember your first night, when it was raining, and you and I walked from the barn to the slahm bus?"

"Yes," he said.

"And do you remember how muddy the road was? You had trouble walking, because you were sinking into the mud."

"Yes," he said, "But it didn't seem to slow you down at all."

"Right," she said, "I reduced my body weight so I could walk on top of the mud."

"But how?" he asked, "It doesn't seem possible."

"How does a brain think?" she countered, "There are so many things about ourselves that we don't understand. We don't really know how a brain thinks, but it does. And we don't really know how we reduce our weight, but we can."

"According to tradition," Alan added, "our ancestors could reduce their body weight enough to fly, but nobody knows for sure if it's true or not. If it is, it was thousands of years ago."

Michael tried to imagine one of the Victorian ladies of Inside flying through the air, but he only managed to picture Mary Poppins, umbrella in hand, sailing stiffly over London.

The area they were passing through was mostly wooded, with an occasional house or farm. They passed a large brick structure labeled Water Department.

"Is that where our drinking water comes from?" Michael asked.

"Mm-hm," Emily nodded. They rode in silence for a while, admiring the magnificent rural scenery. About three quarters of a mile past the Water Department, they reached an intersection, the first they'd encountered since crossing Alexander Avenue in the village. Alan slowed to a stop, giving Michael an opportunity to read the street sign: Digby Street.

They turned right on Digby. As they did so, Michael noticed that just past the intersection, Main Street turned into a dead end. He wondered if that was the northern boundary of Inside. Digby Street took them across the stream via a stone bridge. Just over the bridge, on the right, was a sign identifying Surday Park. A driveway led to a small parking area. Beyond the parking were picnic benches, barbecue pits, and assorted playground equipment.

"Let's set up over there," Emily suggested, pointing to a grassy spot on the side of a small hill. Alan spread out a blanket on the spot, and Emily set down the basket. Sitting on the blanket, Alan immediately removed his shoes and socks and laid back.

"Oh, no you don't!" Emily said, "Not this time! You are not going to sleep through this picnic!"

"I'm not going to sleep," Alan protested, "I'm not the least bit tired."

"You watch," Emily told Michael. "In ten minutes, he'll be sound asleep." Michael laughed as he sat down on the blanket.

"I have no idea what this woman is talking about," Alan told him.

"I give up," said Emily, rolling her eyes and throwing up her hands, "I'm going back to the slahm; I forgot something." Returning to the slahm, she picked up a small book from the front seat. As she started back to the blanket, she realized her bookmark was missing. After a few minutes of fishing around under the seats in the slahm, she located it. Placing it between the pages of her book she once again started back to the blanket, only to find both men asleep. "Well, fine!" she said, "Just fine! OK, go ahead and sleep. I'll just amuse myself." Sitting on a swing, she began to read.

It was ten minutes to four when Alan awoke. Sitting up slowly, he rubbed his eyes and stretched. He looked over at Michael, who was still sleeping, and said, "uh-oh." Looking around, he spied Emily, who was by this time sitting under a tree, still engrossed in her book. Alan reached over and shook Michael. "Wake up," he said, "I think we've in trouble."

Pulling himself into a sitting position, Michael asked, "How long were we asleep?"

"About two and a half hours. It's almost four," he said, showing Michael his watch.

Standing up, Alan said, "Well, I guess we'd better get it over with. Come on." Together they walked over to the tree where Emily sat.

"Emily," Alan began.

"I beg your pardon, sir," she interrupted, "Have we been introduced?"

"Come on, Emily," Michael said.

"Excuse me, sir," she said, "But I don't believe I've made your acquaintance, either. I came here today with two certain gentlemen, but we apparently became separated. You didn't happen to see either of them, did you? One was tall and dumb-looking, and the other was a morally depraved Outsider. My neighbor, Ms. Shea, thinks they're both from Mars. Maybe she's right. Maybe they've gone back to Mars." Her soliloquy completed, she turned her attention once again to her book. She allowed them to stand there awhile, and then casually remarked, "Of course, if they were to apologize..."

Alan and Michael at once fell all over themselves apologizing, while she continued to read.

Finally, she stood, closed the book, and said, "Let's eat!"

"You're not angry anymore?" Alan asked.

"I never really was," she replied, as she walked toward the blanket.

"Then why did you make us stand there so long and apologize like that?" he asked.

"Well," she said, "I had to keep you busy somehow: I only had two pages left to read, and I wasn't about to stop that close to the end."

Alan and Michael stopped walking and looked at each other. "Shall we?" Alan asked.

"Let's!" Michael answered. Running up to Emily, they pulled her to the ground and began to tickle her.

"Help! Murder!" she screamed, "All right, I give up! I give up!" The three lay in the grass, laughing and gasping for breath.

Back at the blanket, Emily took a small mirror out of her purse, and, looking at her hopelessly rumpled coiffure, said, "I don't know how I'm going to explain this to my parents. Heaven only knows what they'll think."

"We could say there was a hurricane," Michael offered.

"There are no hurricanes Inside," she pointed out.

"A crazed bird attacked you?" Alan suggested.

"Too far-fetched," she said.

As the trio ate, Michael and Alan took turns inventing outrageous excuses for Emily's disheveled appearance. They decided to tell the Graes that they were minding their own business, admiring the rainbows in their lemonade, when they were attacked by a Martian with a broom. It wasn't believable, but Emily hoped their sense of humor would override their shock at her appearance.

13

O GOD OUR HELP IN AGES PAST

Emily knelt in front of a bookshelf in the living room looking for another book to read. Michael came down the stairs and asked, "Emily, is there any place where I can have American money exchanged for Inside money? I want to get my suit cleaned for church tomorrow."

"That's a good question," she said, getting up. "I have no idea. Let me call my boss." Picking up the phone, she dialed his number. "Mr. Taravel? Hi, this is Emily. I have a question. Can the bank exchange Outside currency for Sheryls? Oh, uh, huh... One hundred and fifty? OK, I'll tell him. Thanks. See you Monday... No, I won't be late. Bye." Hanging up the phone, she turned to Michael, and said, "The bank can't accept Outside currency because they have no way to use it. But the Seers have opened an account in your name. You have one hundred and fifty Sheryls on deposit."

"Oh," he said, "How much is that? I think your father said a Sheryl is about a dollar and a half."

"It's two hundred and twenty-five dollars," she said.

"You did that fast," Michael said, somewhat awed by her arithmetical prowess.

"Well, the bank didn't hire me because I'm pretty, you know. I was a mathematics major in high school," she boasted.

"Well, you needn't be so proud," Michael said, "I also managed to distinguish myself in the math field."

"Oh?" she said, "Really?"

"Sure," he said, "I managed to get a lower grade in Geometry than anyone else in the entire history of my school. And not only that," he continued, "but I achieved similar 'honors' in Algebra and Chemistry."

"Marvelous," she said in mock admiration, "Did you manage to pass any courses?"

"Well," he smiling, "I did get high honors in French and English. *Prête-moi cinq Sheryls.*"

"What does that mean?" she asked.

"It means 'Lend me five Sheryls.' I need to get my suit cleaned."

"How do you say 'Take a flying leap at the moon' in French?" she asked jokingly, as she took five One Sheryl notes from her purse.

Roughly 3½" x 5", One Sheryl notes are violet in color. There are also ten, fifty and hundred Sheryl notes, also violet. The One Sheryl note has a picture of Markanor, a Seer from the sixteenth century. Because of his picture, the One Sheryl note is sometimes called a Mark, a slang term, used the way "buck" is used for dollar.

At the corner of Main Street and West Alexander Avenue was a coin laundry and dry cleaning establishment. A sign in the window boasted "One Hour Dry Clean & Press." It was past five thirty when Michael finally took his suit to the cleaners. He hoped they would still be open. He was in luck; they were open till nine pm.

"Good afternoon, Mr. London," said the woman who sat behind the counter, as she stood, "What can I do for you?"

"I need to get this suit cleaned and pressed, Miss..." "Ms. Teefel," she said, "But everyone calls me Abby."

"Glad to meet you, Abby."

"Likewise. That's one-fifty for clean and press."

Michael handed her two Sheryl notes, and she gave him a silver-colored, quarter-size coin that said '50 Hibs'. Looking at the coin, he said, "Hibs? Are there a hundred Hibs in a Sheryl?"

"Right," she said, "Here, let me show you." From her cash drawer she took a silver coin, about the size of a dime. "This is one Hib." Next she took a silver coin the size of a nickel, and placed it on the counter next to the first one. "This is ten Hibs, and this," she continued, taking out a coin like the one she had handed Michael in change, "is fifty Hibs."

He examined the coins closely. The numbers were clearly marked, so he knew he'd have no trouble differentiating. Abby placed one more coin on the counter, roughly half-dollar sized.

"This is a one Sheryl coin," she said. The coins were lined up on the counter in size order, with about an inch between each one. Abby placed her hand, palm side down, over the smallest, an inch above the counter. She slowly moved her hand down the row of coins. As her hand covered the second coin, Michael saw that the first one had vanished. As she moved her hand down the row, each coin vanished in turn.

"Hey!" said Michael, "That's pretty good! Where did they go?"

"Go?" she asked, "Nowhere. They're right there." He looked down at the counter again. All except the smallest coin had returned.

"Where's the little one?" he asked.

"You've got it," she said, reaching into his left ear, and drawing out the Hib. "Just a hobby of mine," she said, smiling, "Your suit will be ready in an hour."

The Church of Inside is on Main Street, about a block and a half south of the Graes' house. It was eight forty five a.m. when Michael, Emily, and her parents left the house for church. Walking down Main Street, many of Inside's families, wearing their Sunday best, waved and called 'Good morning' to each other. The church was a large white frame building, modeled after the 'country church' concept. As they neared the church, the bell in the open tower began to ring. Inside the vestibule, a boy of about ten was pulling the bell-rope, and "riding" the rope up, as the weight of the swinging bell pulled him two or three feet into the air.

Entering the sanctuary, Michael saw some familiar faces: Mrs. Enore, wearing an outrageously huge hat, nodded to him, and then made her way to the front pew. Mrs. Bolan stuck her nose in the air, ignored everyone, and followed Mrs. Enore. Others already seated: Abby, Alan, Bryan Veller, Barbara Seal. On the left side near the back, the Glen family sat together.

"Why don't you sit with Hartas?" whispered Mrs. Grae to Michael.

"You won't mind?" he whispered back. She shook her head, smiling, and gently propelled him toward the pew where the Glens were sitting.

"May I join you?" he politely asked Arla Glen. "Of course," she said, "It's good to see you."

There was just time for him to exchange greetings with Hartas and Tom, when a chime rang. Latecomers rushed for seats and the chime sounded again. The congregation stood, and the chime sounded a third time. From a side door near the pulpit, the Seers entered, dressed as they had been when last Michael had seen them. They were followed by their families, and sat in a separate row of pews behind the pulpit. The chime sounded again and Vicar Chelwith entered, wearing a gray suit. Organ music from an unseen source filled the room, and the Vicar called for "Hymn number 231." The rustle of pages was heard as people hurried to find the correct hymn. The Vicar led the singing, and the congregation followed enthusiastically:

O God, our help in ages past,
Our hope for years to come.
Our shelter from the weary blast,
And our eternal home.

Michael knew the song and joined in without hesitation. The second hymn, however, was new to him:

Teach us Thy ways, Show us Thy paths,
O Ancient of Days, reigning in triumph,
Teach us Thy ways.

Following the second hymn, the congregation was seated, and. the Pastor made the announcements. "The Church Cleaning Committee will meet this Thursday evening at 7 pm for a special dinner sponsored by the Church." He flipped through his notes, looking for the next announcement. "The Junior Sunday School Class Choir will be singing for us next Sunday morning. And, last, but not least, on behalf of the Church, I'd like to welcome Michael London. Michael, welcome Inside, and welcome to our Church family." Thoroughly embarrassed, Michael turned a brilliant shade of red. He tried to say 'thank you', but when he opened his mouth, not a sound came out.

Vicar Chelwith preached a sermon on the Good Samaritan. His style was enthusiastic, and he had no trouble holding the attention of all present. A short period of prayer and meditation followed, during which the Vicar was handed a note. With a smile he stood and announced, "I'm told that one of our Sunday School children would like to sing for us." A tiny girl with two red pigtails sticking up, and a face that suggested mischief, entered, running, through the same door the Seers had used. "This is Lisa," said Vicar Chelwith, "She's five years old, and is in the Nursery class."

Lisa stood in front of the pulpit, the picture of self-confidence... until she looked at the congregation. With one hand grasping the hem of her dress, and the other in her mouth, she stood silent.

"Go ahead!" whispered an unseen person behind the door.

"I forgot," she whispered back with three fingers in her mouth.

"My name is Lisa..." coached the invisible voice.

"Oh, yeah!" the child said, "I know! My name is Lisa, and..." The fingers went back in her mouth.

"...and I would like to sing..." whispered her prompter.

"...and I would like to sing a song..." Fingers again.

"for..." said the doorway.

"a song for... for... him!" she blurted out, pointing at Michael. As the congregation laughed, she stuck her fingers back in her mouth.

"Go ahead!" coached the whisperer.

"I forgot," she said through her fingers.

"Jesus loves me..."

"I know!" she said. Now clutching the hem of her dress with both hands, she sang, *"Jesus loves me, this I know..."* As she sang the well-known hymn, she was, without realizing it, pulling her dress higher and higher, as little girls sometimes will.

As the dress rose to embarrassing heights, the door said, "Oh, Lord!" and Vicar Chelwith's wife rushed out and pulled Lisa's dress back to its proper length. Lisa, her song over, stuck out her lip and glared at Mrs. Tey.

"Lisa," the woman said, "a lady doesn't pull her dress up like that."

"I'm not a lady!" the child asserted, sticking out her tongue and running out the side door. Quickly reappearing, she said, "I forgot... Welcome Inside, Mr. London!" With another sticking out of her tongue at Mrs. Tey, she was gone.

Mrs. Tey, following the girl out, turned to the congregation and asked, "Anyone want to buy a slightly used Sunday School class?"

14

THE SECRET

Monday morning had arrived, and Michael and the Grae family sat eating breakfast. Or, rather, the Graes ate; Michael toyed with his scrambled eggs.

"Michael," Mrs. Grae said, "You're not eating! What's wrong?"

"Nothing," he answered with a cryptic smile. "I'm not very hungry. May I be excused?"

"Well, of course," she said, rather puzzled. But before she could frame another question, Michael was gone, taking the stairs to his room two at a time.

"He's up to something," Mrs. Grae said, half to her husband and daughter, and half to herself. "I know that look. It's the same one you get when you're plotting something, Gene."

Her husband smiled, but said nothing. Moments later, Michael returned, running down the stairs, with a small, green overnight bag in hand. He was heading for the front door when Mrs. Grae issued a command:

"Hold it right there, young man!"

He froze in his tracks, and then turned to see the woman coming towards him, armed with a glass of tomato juice.

"Drink this," she ordered. Looking at the overnight bag, she added, "I won't ask. Will you be home for lunch?"

"Yes, ma'am," he said, handing her the now empty glass. As he left, he overheard Mrs. Grae, again half addressing her family and half addressing herself: *"The boy would starve if I let him. No wonder he ate so much his first day here: He probably hadn't bothered to eat for a week. I'll never understand..."* That was all he heard. He was going to the Hall of Seers.

It was only eight thirty-five when he opened the door to the white brick building. The man in knickers led him to a beautifully furnished waiting room. Sitting in an overstuffed Victorian chair, he looked around at the pictures that lined the walls. They appeared to be photographs, black and white, of men and women wearing the robes of Seers. Standing up, he moved closer to the wall to see better. The first picture was of a woman with long, straight hair. The name 'Mornine' was written on the plaque below the picture, followed by the notation '1520-1595.' Moving to the right, he read the name on the next one. 'Marcus,' with the dates '1742-1764.' The picture was of a young man in his late teens. The sadness in the young Seer's eyes was evident, and Michael wondered what tragic fate (Seghva?) had befallen the boy. He made a mental note to check the library for a book on young Marcus. At nine a.m., Michael was ushered into the presence of the Seers.

"Good morning, Michael," Telesina said, rising. "You have three topics to discuss with us."

"I do?" Michael asked. He could only think of one.

"Certainly," Telesina said. "We'll take the easiest first: You want to know where the Public Library is. Head south on Main Street. A half block past the Church, turn right on Southton Street. The Library is the second building on the right."

Michael stood awestruck. "Thank you," he managed to whisper.

"Next," the Seer continued, "you want to ask us about Ms. Shea. Melfina will explain." Melfina rose as Telesina sat down.

"Michael," he began, "We are somewhat familiar with the customs of Outsiders. No doubt it seems cruel to you that Ms. Shea is allowed to stay the way she is, without benefit of medical treatment. And it probably seems more cruel that many people treat Ms. Shea as humorous." He paused a moment to think, and then continued. "Perhaps the best thing to do is start at the beginning." Closing his eyes, Melfina stretched his right arm out toward the side of the room. Suddenly, where there had been darkness, light came out, and a picture of a rundown farm appeared. The image wasn't exactly like a movie screen, but more three-dimensional. Michael felt like he could reach right out and touch the farmhouse or barn.

Melfina began to speak. "This is where Ms. Shea was born. She wasn't Shea yet; her name was Letitia Cern. Her family called her Tish. She was the youngest of five children." As he spoke, the farmhouse door opened, and a little girl came running out, crying. The child, about four years old, ran toward the barn. "That's Tish," Melfina said. "Her father just died. Of the five children, she was closest to him."

The image faded, and a new picture took its place: A girl of about thirteen years, on her knees, scrubbing a kitchen floor. Her two long, red braids nearly reached the wet floor. She wore a dirty gray blouse and a black skirt with a torn hem. Her feet were bare.

"Mrs. Cern couldn't keep the farm going. She sold it, and bought a small house on the east side of the village. Unfortunately, she died less than a year later. Letitia and the other children were forced to leave school and find work. Tish scrubbed floors and washed clothes from age five until she married, at age eighteen."

Again the picture faded, and the new image was the front door of the Church. A crowd of people stood outside in formal attire. A more grown-up Tish appeared in the doorway wearing a wedding gown, with a handsome young man holding her hand. "This is Mark Shea," the Seer continued. "Things were finally looking up for Letitia. Mark had a good job, and had inherited his parents' large home on the west side of the village."

The picture blurred and then cleared. The scene was again the Church. The crowd seemed to be the same people, but no one was smiling. Letitia again appeared in the doorway. She wore a black dress and a black veil obscured her face. She wiped her eyes with a white handkerchief, a stark contrast to her dismal attire. She cried openly, and Michael noticed that several in the crowd also wept.

Feeling a lump building in his throat, Michael whispered, "Mark?"Melfina nodded silently. "How long...," Michael tried to ask.

The Seer, understanding the question, answered, "Three years. No children. She never remarried."

"What did she do?" Michael asked.

"She scrubbed floors again," Melfina said, as the image changed to a woman of about fifty years, on her knees, scrub brush in hand.

"What about her brothers and sisters?" Michael asked. "Didn't they help her?"

"They did what they could, but they were no better off than she was," Melfina explained. "Letitia outlived them all. Her only living relative is her niece, Alora. Alora Cern is the only daughter of Letitia's brother, Samuel. Alora used to be married to Dr. Henry Whitstone. She now lives with her Aunt Tish."

"Couldn't you do anything to help her?" Michael asked.

"I know what you're thinking, Michael," Melfina answered. "But you must understand, as Seers, we have the ability to *know* a person's future. But we cannot *create* that future. We are not God. We couldn't stop her parents or husband from dying. But we did what we could: When the last of her siblings died, we allowed her to lose touch with a portion of reality. We helped her escape from some of the pain. Ms. Shea is happier now than she has ever been before. To take that away from her now would be the worst cruelty. Don't be afraid to laugh at her: All her life she has known tears; she needs the laughter. It keeps her young and alive. It's the childhood she never had." Melfina lowered his arm, and the wall was darkness again. He resumed his seat as Telesina rose again.

"You had one further matter to discuss," the Seer began. "May we see the statue?"

"You know about the statue?" Michael asked, his voice showing his surprise.

"Of course," said Telesina. "But we would like to see it."

Reaching into his overnight bag, Michael removed the miniature Hildegarde Bolan, and placed it on the desk, facing the Seers. The three men leaned forward to view the object more closely. For a moment there was silence, and then the quiet was broken by laughter. First Harmor, then Telesina, then Melfina, quietly at first, but soon all three Seers roared with laughter. Tears streamed down their faces, and Harmor nearly fell out of his seat. "I... can't...breathe!" one of them gasped through his laughter. Gradually, they regained their composure, but upon inspecting the statue again, the laughter was renewed.

Michael watched the scene with great amusement. This wasn't exactly the reaction he had expected, but he was glad they appreciated the humor of the figure. He hoped they would also appreciate the value.

His face red from laughing, Telesina wiped the last of the tears from his eyes, and stood up straight again. "We think it's a wonderful idea," he said.

"But I haven't asked you yet," Michael protested.

"Oh, very well," the Seer said. "Go ahead."

"I know you already know what I want to do, but I'll feel better if I can say it. Hartas has made dozens of statues like this. Mr. Grae said that a statue like this would sell for fifty Sheryls."

"Easily," Telesina interjected, the other Seers nodding in assent.

"It's no secret that Hartas' poor self-image is more of a problem than his size. I think these statues could be the answer to that problem. If people wanted to buy his statues, he would soon realize that if his work has value, he does, too. Is there some way that we could get him started?"

"Well," Telesina said, rubbing his chin thoughtfully, "Hartas has no business experience. He'd need someone to manage the business for him..."

"Well..." Michael began.

"You're hired!" Telesina interrupted. Stretching out his hand, he gave Michael a skeleton key.

"What's this?" Michael asked him.

"Do you know the vacant store on Center Lane, next to the bookstore?" Telesina asked. As Michael nodded, the Seer continued, "Well, that's the key. We've been saving the store for Hartas. Oh, here," he said, handing Michael some papers. "This is the deed to the store. It's in the name of Hartas Glen and Michael London."

"You mean you're giving it to us?" Michael asked incredulously.

"Well, yes," Telesina said. "Hartas' father worked for the town for many years. Let's say this is our way of saying 'thank you' posthumously. I know he would be pleased with such an opportunity for his son. Of course, you'll still have to approach Hartas with the idea. I don't think that will be a problem, though. He trusts you."

15

THE SECRET, CONTINUED

It was ten thirty when Michael left the Hall of Seers. Stepping outside, his eyes were stabbed by the bright sunlight, and he raised his hand to shield them. In his mind, he was forming a strategy for talking Hartas into opening a business. His first order of business was to get some money. The bank was about a block west. As he entered the cool lobby, he said a mental 'thank you' to the Deity for His wonderful miracle of air conditioning. There were about six or seven people waiting in line to transact their business with the three tellers.

"Good morning, Mr. London," the young teller said. "My name is Jon. How may I help you?"

"Um, I'm told I have an account here," Michael said.

"That's right," Jon agreed, punching some buttons on his computer terminal. "Your balance is one hundred and fifty Sheryls. Would you like to make a withdrawal?"

"Yes," Michael answered, "but I need to ask a couple of strange questions first, OK?"

Jon smiled, and said, "Sure."

"Can you tell me the name of a very good restaurant?" Michael asked, a little embarrassed by his own question.

"No problem," Jon answered. "Do you know where Mrs. Enore lives?"

"Yes," said Michael, nodding.

"Well, right around the corner on Colby Boulevard is the Druid House. Their food is excellent."

"Great," Michael said. "Now, strange question number two: How much would I need for dinner for two?"

"About thirty five Sheryls should do it," Jon said. "It won't be that much, but it's better to have too much than not enough."

"All right," said Michael. "Then I need to take out forty Sheryls. I owe Emily Grae five. Would you be able to give it to her for me?"

"Sure," Jon said. "Withdraw forty, five to Emily, and thirty five to you. Anything else?"

"No, thank you," Michael said, taking his money. "I appreciate your help."

"My pleasure. Have a good morning."

Next stop was Hartas' house. Sitting on the Glen's front steps, Michael took Mrs. Bolan out of the overnight bag and handed her to Hartas.

"Are you finished with it?" Hartas asked, cradling the figure in his hands.

"Mm-hmm," Michael assented.

"And?" Hartas asked, expectantly.

"And?" Michael echoed.

"You're not going to tell me what you're up to?" Hartas asked, disappointment in his voice.

"Of course I'll tell you," Michael said. "But not here. We have to have a very serious talk. Would you like to have dinner tonight at the Druid House? My treat."

Hartas' face lit up like a spotlight. "The Druid House? Really? You're not kidding?"

"No, I'm not kidding," Michael said. "Have you ever eaten there before?"

"No," said Hartas, "never. How can you afford it?"

"That's a secret," Michael said with a wink and a smile. "I'll tell you my whole crazy idea tonight while we eat. OK?"

"OK," Hartas agreed, still not sure he was hearing right. "I hope my suit still fits."

"I'll pick you up at six thirty," Michael said, as got up and started home.

Hartas sat for a long time staring at the statue in his hands. "If only you could talk..." Suddenly he leaped up and ran inside. "Hey, Mom, guess what!"

"Well, it's the mystery man!" said Mrs. Grae, as Michael came into the kitchen. "Do you want to let me in on the secret?"

He smiled at her a minute, and then answered, "Not yet. Tonight. I won't be here for dinner. I'm taking Hartas to the Druid House for dinner. When I get back, I promise I'll tell you the whole story. I can't say anything now, because I haven't spoken to Hartas about it yet."

"Oh," said Mrs. Grae in a knowing tone, but her face betrayed her confusion. "The part about dinner sounds nice, but I wouldn't tell Emily you're taking Hartas. She's not ready to think 'Hartas Glen' and 'Druid House' in the same thought; the shock would kill her!"

"OK," Michael agreed with a chuckle. "Do I need to make a reservation?"

"It would be a good idea," she said. "They're pretty popular, and have been known to run out of tables."

"Good afternoon, Druid House. May I help you?" queried the female voice on the phone.

"I'd like to make a reservation for a party of two for dinner at seven."

"Party of two, seven p.m. What name, please?" she asked.

"Michael London," he answered.

"Very good, Mr. London. Reservation confirmed for this evening. Oh, by the way, welcome Inside."

"Thank you," he said, blushing as he hung up the phone, and simultaneously feeling silly for blushing.

All during lunch, Emily stared first at Michael, then at her mother. He pretended not to notice, while Mrs. Grae just smiled. After a while, totally exasperated, Emily blurted out, "Well, fine! Fine! Keep me in the dark! Don't tell me what's going on!"

"Going on?" Mrs. Grae asked innocently. "What are you talking about?"

"Hmph!" she said. "I'm going to be late for work." Without another word, she was gone.

"It's only twenty after twelve," Mrs. Grae remarked. "She'll be early getting back. I do hope she doesn't let Mr. Taravel see her. If he sees that she's early, he'll think she's ill!"

The sign over the doorway said 'Public Library' in the old Roman style, so that 'PUBLIC' was spelled 'PVBLIC.'

"May I help you, Mr. London?" asked the elderly man seated at the reference desk. "I'm Mr. Halton, the librarian."

"Yes," Michael answered. "I was interested in finding out about Seers who lived a long time ago."

"If you'll follow me," the librarian said, rising, and leading the way to a shelf of reference books, "I have a book that will help you. This is the Encyclopedia of Seers." He pulled a large volume down from the shelf. Placing it on a table, he motioned for Michael to sit. "All the Seers are listed in alphabetical order. After the name is a biographical section, one to three paragraphs. If there is a separate book about that Seer, it will be noted at the end of the biography. If you have any questions, just ask." Before Michael could thank him, he was gone, hurrying back to his desk.

Michael sat down and opened the immense book. 'Good,' he thought, 'there are pictures.' Above each name was a portrait of that Seer. He turned to Marcus, the Seer whose picture had intrigued him that morning. To his dismay, he found that there were quite a few Seers named Marcus, with only dates of birth and death to further distinguish them. He couldn't remember the dates of the Marcus he was looking for, but he remembered the face, the eyes. He flipped through the pages until he found the Marcus he was looking for: Marcus, 1742-1764. The biography followed:

"Marcus was born in the North American Inside on June 27, 1742. He was the son of Seer Isabella and Mr. Alfred Colby. In 1750, when Marcus was eight years old, Seer Isabella died, and he became the second youngest Seer in the history of the North American Inside. (The youngest was Seer Elizabeth, 1602-1680, q.v.)

Seer Marcus was noted for his compassion for others, his wisdom, and his poems, some of which were published in 1760, when he was eighteen years of age. Marcus suffered from a rare disorder known as Fredo Kodme, or Seers' Plague. Although only five Seers have died of the affliction, it has never been known to strike anyone who wasn't a Seer. There is no known cure. Seer Marcus' mother was one of those afflicted. She was twenty-seven when she died.

Marcus knew his Seghva included death at age twenty-two, and the knowledge caused him great sadness. This sadness can be seen in the above portrait, the only known likeness of the Seer. It is also evident in his poetry. Seer Marcus died June 20th, 1764, just a week short of twenty-two years. His nineteen year old sister, Lisa, became Seer in his stead. (See Lisa, 1746-1810)

Other books: Poems of Seer Marcus 1742-1764, available in the original Fortu and also in English translation."

When Michael left the library, he took with him two things. One was a book of poems by Seer Marcus, and the other was a feeling of sadness for the young Seer.

16

PARTNERSHIP

It was just six thirty when Michael stepped onto the Glen's front porch and knocked on the door.

"Michael," said Arla Glen, as she opened the door. "You look magnificent. Please come in. Hartas is almost ready."

"Thank you, Mrs. Glen," he said, stepping inside. "How are you?"

"Oh," she replied, "I'm well, thank you."

"I'm ready," Hartas called out. A moment later, he appeared, quite a figure in his formal black attire. "How do I look?"

For a moment, no one spoke. "Oh, Hartas!" his mother said at last. "What a fine young man! Doesn't he look grand, Michael?" she asked.

"Incredible," Michael said, awestruck by the transformation. Could this be the same Hartas Glen who was turning somersaults on the Village Green the other day? This? This powerfully handsome little man, with not a spot of dirt on his clothing, not a hair out of place?

"Do you like it?" he asked Michael. "The suit, I mean."

"Yes," said Michael, with obvious admiration.

"It's the suit I wore when..." he paused, looking at his mother. "...when Daddy died. I was only about an inch shorter then. Mom fixed it so it would fit again."

"You look great," Michael said, "really!"

"Well, I guess I'm ready," Hartas said. "Bye, Mom." He gave her a peck on the cheek.

"Bye, Mrs. Glen," Michael said. "We won't be too late." "Have a good time, boys," the woman said, as she closed the front door behind them. Michael wasn't sure, but for a split second before the door closed, he thought he saw tears in her eyes.

From the outside, the Druid House was unremarkable: a one-story brick structure painted white, with heavy curtains in the windows. A sign next to the door identified the establishment and requested proper attire.

"Mr. London," said the rather heavy-set woman who guarded the entrance to the dining room. "It is a great honor. I am Felicity Varton, owner of the Druid House. When I heard you were coming, I insisted on greeting you myself. I'm so pleased..." For the first time she noticed Hartas standing next to Michael. "Is... this... I mean... Mr. Glen, isn't it?" she stuttered.

"That's right," Michael answered for Hartas, who was feeling very out of place. "Mr. Glen and I will be dining together this evening," he continued with polite formality.

"Very good," the woman replied, having regained her composure. "Please follow me." She led them into the dining room, which seemed full, there being at least thirty people dining. In a small alcove was a table for two. Removing a 'reserved' sign, she motioned for them to be seated. "Your waiter will be with you shortly... Um, Mr. Glen, I'd like to apologize... I mean, I was just surprised..." She blushed red as she tried to explain. "I... well, I'm sorry. Please enjoy your dinner. Excuse me." With that, she was gone.

"Good evening, Gentlemen. My name is Mark. I'll be your waiter. Mrs. Varton has asked me to tell you that your dinner tonight will be compliments of the house."

As they waited for their dinner, Michael outlined his plan. Hartas listened in silence until he was finished.

"I don't know, Michael. Who'd want my statues?"

"But that's the best part: Not only will people want them, but they'll be willing to pay for them. Fifty Sheryls or more for one statue."

Hartas looked at him doubtfully. "Come on," he said. "Fifty Sheryls? Who told you that?"

"Two people," Michael answered. "Mr. Grae..."

"He was probably just kidding," Hartas interrupted.

"...and Telesina," Michael finished.

At the mention of the Seer's name, Hartas' expression changed. His eyes widened, and he looked up, his eyes meeting Michael's. "Telesina? Are you sure?"

"Telesina," Michael repeated, "and Harmor and Melfina agreed."

Hartas just shook his head in amazement. At length he asked, "How will we sell them?"

"Now you're talking!" Michael exclaimed. "The Seers suggested a partnership. You carve the statues, and I'll handle the business aspect. And we'll split the profits, any percentage you like. Sound OK, so far?"

"Uh-huh," Hartas agreed, nodding.

"Good," Michael said. "The Seers gave us a little something to get us started. I'll show you after dinner."

Following an exceptionally good meal of Chicken Rosemary, parslied potatoes, steamed broccoli with butter sauce, and French vanilla ice cream for dessert, the two prepared to leave. Per Mrs. Varton's instructions, Mark refused to allow them to pay for dinner. "Please come see us again soon," he said as they left.

"Where are we going?" Hartas asked.

"I want to show you what the Seers gave us," Michael replied. When they reached Center Lane, they paused in front of the empty store. The adjoining bookstore was closed, so there wasn't much light to see by. "There it is," Michael announced triumphantly.

"Oh, it's beautiful," Hartas said flatly. "What am I supposed to be looking at?"

"Well, what do you see?" Michael asked him.

"Nothing. An empty store."

"Right," Michael said.

"An empty store?" Hartas asked uncomprehendingly. "Ohhh, an empty store!" he said, as the understanding dawned. "You don't mean they gave this to us?"

To answer his question, Michael reached into his pocket and held up the key for Hartas to see.

"I don't know what to say," Hartas gasped. "Our own store!"

"Partners?" Michael asked, extending his right hand.

"Partners!" Hartas said, shaking Michael's hand.

At ten o'clock, Michael returned to the Graes' house. Gene and Marbel were in the dining room, reading the newspaper and occasionally fighting over the various sections. They enjoyed reading the paper together, and their mock-arguments over it were half the fun. As Michael entered the living room, they looked up from their reading, and Emily shouted from upstairs, "Is that him?" Without waiting for an answer, she descended rapidly. Cornering him in the doorway between the living room and dining room, she planted her hands firmly on her hips. "Well?" she demanded.

"Sit down," he said, amused by her attitude. "I've got some news," he began, as he guided Emily toward a dining room chair. In his left hand he carried a small object wrapped in a shirt. "Mr. Grae," he said, unwrapping the shirt, "you've already seen this. I borrowed it again so the rest of the family could see it." From the shirt he withdrew the statue of Hildegarde Bolan and set it on the table between Emily and her mother. Placing his finger on his lips, he signaled Mr. Grae not to reveal any information about the object. The reaction of the two women to the statue was predictable, and Michael waited patiently for both to stop laughing and catch their breath.

"Who made this?" Emily squealed, her breathing again under control.

"Before I tell you," Michael answered, "let me tell you the news. Do you know the empty store on Center Lane?" They nodded and he continued. "Soon you will be able to buy statues like this one at that store. There will be statues of people, animals and buildings, all carved by hand." He paused, and then said, "These statues are carved by my business partner."

"Business partner," Emily said. "Who?"

Michael and Mr. Grae exchanged knowing looks, and then he said, "Why don't you ask your father?"

"Daddy?" Emily said, looking at her father. "You know?"

The older man smiled. "Yes, I know. But look at the statue. See how well it's made? It's good, don't you think?"

"It's beautiful, Dad, but..."

"And the artist is obviously gifted, wouldn't you say, Emily?"

"Obviously. Very talented. But who is it?"

"Yes, Gene," Mrs. Grae interjected. "Tell us!"

With a smile at Michael, he announced, "This marvelous piece is part of a large collection hand carved by Hartas Glen."

Emily looked at the statue again, and fainted.

17

A LESSON FOR EMILY

'Hartas' Figurines' read the sign over the door. In the store windows, a large collection of statues was decoratively displayed. It had been three months since Michael and Hartas opened their doors for business, and the statues were selling at an incredible rate. Ever since Celeste Enore had purchased one and declared the creations *de rigueur* for home décor, the demand had tripled. Everyone had to have at least one Hartas original. People as important as Harmor, the Vicar, and Mr. Taravel had commissioned Hartas to carve statues of their wives. This started the tradition of giving the figurines as gifts for birthdays, anniversaries, etc.

The effect of all this on Hartas was profound. Never had he felt so good about himself. For the first time in his life, he felt like he had value. No longer a pest to ignore, he had become something of a celebrity. On the streets, people spoke to him. They called him 'Mr. Glen.' He, Hartas Glen, had become a person.

It was Saturday morning. Emily Grae was sitting on her front porch, diligently trying to crochet. Hartas was at the store rearranging the window display. Business was slow that morning, so Michael took the opportunity to cross the Green to talk with Emily.

"Good morning. Am I intruding?" he asked.

"Please do," she replied, trying to unravel the knots she had created. "I'll never get the hang of this."

Michael sat opposite her, and for a moment, watched in silent amusement as she tried to pull out the stitches. At length, he spoke. "I think we should talk."

She put down her tangles and looked at him. "Yes," she agreed. "We should."

"What do you have against Hartas?" he asked.

For a moment, she didn't answer. She picked up her crochet hook and re-inspected the knots. Putting it down, she broke the silence. "It isn't Hartas, exactly," she began. "I thought it was, but it isn't."

"Then what is it?" he asked.

"I don't know how to explain it," she said.

"Let me try," Michael said. "I think I can understand what you are feeling. Outside, we have large ships called ocean liners. I don't know how these things work today, but it used to be that the passengers were divided into classes. First class was reserved for the very rich. Second class was for those who weren't rich, but weren't poor either. Third class was for the very poor. First class passengers had the best of everything: the best food, private rooms, expensive décor, the works. But third class passengers slept in rooms with four or more people. Their dining rooms had long tables with benches, and the food wasn't good. If there was an emergency, first class was rescued first. Third was last, if they were rescued at all."

Emily listened to this point, and then interrupted. "But what does that have to do with us?"

"I'm getting to that," he said. "Let me finish. This separation of classes was taken very seriously. The classes didn't mingle.

A first class passenger would never associate with a third class passenger. The first class seemed to actually believe that the third class people were inferior. But Outside society began to realize that it wasn't true. Higher social status and financial standing don't make a person superior. I think Inside is like those ocean liners. First class is the rich people, the west side of the village. Third class is the poor people on the east side. Your family has always been first class. They usually have little contact with the poorer class. I think perhaps Hartas has been for you a symbol of the third class. Now you see your symbol crossing class lines, and it confuses you. Does that make sense?" She didn't answer. "Emily?"

Without a word she jumped up and started to run down Main Street toward Colby Boulevard. Michael rose to follow, but a hand on his shoulder stopped him. He turned to see Mr. Grae.

"Let her go, son," he said. "You did your part: You told her the truth. The rest is up to her."

It was two o'clock. As the Town Hall clock struck the hour, Michael looked up from the counter where he stood adding the morning's sales on a calculator. He couldn't seem to get the numbers to add up properly. All he could think about was Emily. Had he been too blunt? Maybe he should have suggested a visit to the Seers. He looked at the calculator again. Clearing the machine, he tried again to enter the figures correctly. As he did so, the door opened slowly. He glanced up from his work to see Emily peering in.

"May I come in?" she inquired timidly.

"Of course," he answered quickly. He opened his mouth to speak again, but she help up her hand.

"Please," she said, "let me say this. When we talked this morning, I got angry. I was angrier than I can ever remember being. I felt like you had no right to say those things to me, like you were calling me a snob. I was so furious that I had to get away. I went to talk to Alan. To yell at him, actually. He let me rant and rave for at least half an hour. I'm glad you weren't there. Some of the things I said were unforgivable. When I finally calmed down enough to think straight, I realized something: The reason I was so angry was because you were right." Again, Michael tried to speak, but she held up her hand to retain the floor. "Please," she said, "I've got to finish this. I owe you an apology... I'm sorry." She paused and then asked, "Is Hartas here?"

"He's in the back," Michael said, pointing to the curtained doorway behind him.

"Hartas!" she called out.

"Yeah?" came the reply.

"Hartas, could you come out for a moment?" A few seconds later, he appeared, his clothes and hair covered with wood shavings. "Hartas," she said, "I owe you an apology."

"You do?" he asked incredulously.

"Yes. For as long as I can remember, I've treated you... well, you know what I mean. I'm really sorry. If you'll forgive me, I'd like us to be friends."

Hartas was dumbfounded. At first, he expected her to burst out laughing. But after making eye contact, he realized she was serious.

"Forgive me?" she asked again. He nodded slowly, his vocal abilities gone. She smiled, stuck out her hand and said, "Are we friends?"

Taking her hand, he returned her smile. "We are!" he said.

Thank you," she said. Turning to Michael, she added, "And thank *you*. I feel wonderful!" Lowering her body weight, she waltzed out on tiptoe, barely touching the ground.

The two men watched her leave, and Hartas said, "If this is a dream, please don't wake me up."

The high point of Hartas' social climb came the day the impossible happened. It started with the phone call:

"Hartas' Figurines. Hartas Glen speaking. May I help you?"

"Mr. Glen," began the female caller, "This is Regina, Celeste Enore's maid."

"Yes?"

"Mrs. Enore is having a formal dinner party this evening. Will you be able to attend?"

18

A MEMORY

Michael sat on the Graes' porch, looking across the Green. It was night. The only lights were street lamps and the clock on the Town Hall.

"Michael?" It was Emily. She stepped out onto the porch wearing a pale blue robe over her nightgown. "It's three in the morning. What are you doing?" she asked.

"I couldn't sleep," he said as she sat next to him.

"Something on your mind?" she asked.

"Mm-hmm," he said, nodding.

"Do you want to talk about it?"

He didn't answer right away. "I don't know," he said at length. "I guess I was just missing..." He paused.

"Outside?" she suggested.

"No," he answered truthfully. "I don't miss Outside at all."

"Then you miss... Jeremy, don't you?" He nodded and sighed. "Tell me about him," she asked. "What was he like?"

He smiled as he thought of Jeremy. "You'd have liked him," he said.

"Why?" she asked, prompting him to talk.

"He kind of looked like you."

"He looked like me?" she repeated.

"Well, he had red hair."

"Oh," she said. "Tell me more about him."

"Well, he was twenty-eight years old. He worked at a television station. Do you know about television?"

"Um, radio with pictures, right?"

"Yeah," he said smiling. "That's about right. I met him at a party about three and a half years ago. I'll never forget how his eyes sparkled. They were green, like the sea. You know, I don't even remember what he was wearing; all I saw were his eyes. It was about a week later that my parents were killed in a fire. When I got the news, I sort of fell apart. I don't know why I called Jeremy. I hadn't seen him since the party, and I hardly knew him. But when I called, he came right over. I was a wreck. I couldn't even think straight. He was so calm. He knew just what to do. He made the funeral arrangements, everything. I don't know what I would have done without him. He was always like that, so calm in a crisis. He always knew what to do." He stopped, and for a few minutes they sat in silence. The Town Hall clock struck the half hour.

"How did he die?" Emily asked quietly.

"Cancer," he said, looking away. "Cancer... of everything." He was crying now. "We didn't even know he was sick. We didn't know anything was wrong at all. And then... it was too late. He was gone. Just like that. Gone." Emily put her arms around him as he wept.

19

A MIRACLE

"Dr. Whitstone will see you now, Mr. London."

Michael followed the young woman down a corridor and into a small office. Dr. Whitstone was seated behind the desk. Motioning for Michael to take a seat, he said, "Thank you, Sarah." The woman withdrew, closing the door. "What can I do for you, Michael?"

"Can you tell me about Hartas Glen? I mean why he's short."

"Of course," the doctor said, turning to take a book from the shelf behind him. "First let me explain how the growth process works for Insiders." He opened to a page with a multi-colored representation of a brain. "This is what an Insider's brain looks like," he explained. "It's somewhat different from the brain of an Outsider. I was able to make comparisons because the Seers were kind enough to supply me with medical texts and anatomy charts from Outside when you first arrived. Now this structure here," he said, pointing with a pen to a small section near the base of the brain, "controls growth. Normally, this gland releases growth hormone at a steady rate until a person reaches adulthood. At that time, it shrinks and eventually disappears. This same gland also triggers the onset of puberty at the appropriate time. Now, Hartas stopped growing within a year of his father's death. His mother brought him in for a checkup. All of his physical tests were normal, with one exception: This gland had completely ceased functioning. It didn't atrophy or disappear, it simply became dormant."

"But why?" Michael asked.

"That's the interesting part," the doctor said, closing his textbook. "As I said, all the other physical tests were normal. But his psychological tests were significant. As you are probably aware, stress can have an enormous impact on the functioning of the physical body. In Hartas' case, the shock of his father's death apparently caused the gland to stop functioning. There wasn't anything that could be done about it at that time."

"At that time? You mean it's treatable now?" Michael asked.

"Yes. It's something I stumbled across quite accidentally a couple of years ago. I wanted to start right away, but the Seers intervened, asking me to keep the treatment secret until the proper time. Just this morning, I received word from them that I might begin treatment. Clearly, they knew you would be coming to see me about this. If you would like to discuss it with Hartas, we could start tomorrow morning."

Hartas sat quietly for a long time. "Grow?" Again, silence. "I don't know... what to say. It's been so many years. Will it really make me grow again?"

It was decided that they would keep the treatments secret, even from Mrs. Glen. That way, if they didn't work, no one would be disappointed but Hartas and Michael. At nine the next morning, the two sat in an examining room while Dr. Whitsone explained the procedure.

"Once a week, I will give you an injection. This injection is a concentrated form of the growth hormone your body stopped producing. We will continue treatment for six months, and you should reach full height within a year. But I must warn you; there will be some side effects. We are compressing twelve or more years' worth of growth into only one year. This will put a tremendous strain on your system. You may have sharp pains in your bones, especially your arms and legs. Also, this high a concentration of growth hormone might trigger severe headaches. I thought about lowering the dosage, and prolonging the treatment over a longer period of time, but the results wouldn't be the same, so I decided against it."

"Doctor," Hartas said, "how tall..."

"How tall will you be?"

Hartas nodded.

"I can't say exactly, but there's every reason to believe you'll top six feet."

Hartas rubbed his arm and winced in pain.

"If you had relaxed your arm like he told you, it wouldn't still hurt," Michael reproached. "Now hold still."

"That's easy for you to say," Hartas countered. "He wasn't aiming that needle at your arm.

The two men were in the back room of their store. Hartas stood with his back to the wall, while Michael marked his height with a pencil. Then, using a tape measure, he checked the distance from the floor to the mark.

"Three feet, six inches," he announced.

"I could have told you that," Hartas said dryly, as Michael wrote the numbers next to the mark.

"Well, now you don't have to. We'll check your height each week."

"But it will be at least three weeks before the shots do anything," Hartas protested.

"It won't hurt to check anyway," Michael insisted.

The doctor was wrong about one thing: The first shot did do something: By that afternoon, Hartas had the worst headache he could ever remember having. A call to Dr. Whitstone resulted in a promise for medication.

"I'm surprised you reacted so quickly," the doctor said. "But it's a good sign, actually. The headache indicates that your body recognizes the hormone. I'll send something over to relieve the pain. Do you want it sent to the store or to your house?"

Less than twenty minutes later, a little freckle-faced boy entered the store. He put a small bottle of pills on the counter. "These are for Mr. Glen," he told Michael.

"Thank you," the man answered. "What's your name?"

"Tommy," the boy said, staring at Michael with intense curiosity. "Are you the man from Outside?" he asked.

Michael smiled. "That's right, Tommy. My name is Michael."

"Hello," the boy said, still staring at Michael. The dark hair seemed to fascinate him.

"Here you go, Tommy," Michael said, handing him a one Sheryl coin. "Thanks for bringing the pills over."

The boy's eyes widened when he saw the coin. "Thanks, mister!" he said, as he turned to go. From outside the store, he waved, and Michael waved back.

"I hope Dr. Whitstone's growth hormone works better than his pain killers," Hartas said as he unlocked the store the following morning.

"Still have a headache?" Michael asked, following him inside.

"Yeah, but that's not the worst part. When Mom found out I had a headache, she made a pot of that nasty tea she makes. She's convinced it will cure everything from a cold to leprosy."

"Will it?" Michael asked with a chuckle.

"Who knows?" Hartas replied. "If it tastes half as bad to a germ as it does to me, it'll probably cure anything."

The headaches came and went, some lasting only a few minutes, others a few days. Michael put a foldaway cot in the back room of the store, so Hartas could rest when the headaches came. It was the day after the third treatment that the bone pains began. It started as an uncomfortable sensation in his lower arms. As the day wore on, the feeling became more painful. By evening, his legs, too, were affected.

"It's weird," he said to Michael. "I can't localize the pain. It's not in one part. The entire bones are hurting. I can feel the exact shape of each bone that hurts."

Mercifully, these pains, like the headaches, were intermittent. So far, there had been no change in his height. The fourth injection also brought no change, just more pain. The day of the fifth shot, Michael again forced Hartas to stand against the wall in the store.

"This is a waste of time, Michael," he protested. "Don't you think I'd know if I had grown?"

"Stand still," was all Michael said for a moment. Then, "Well... Well!"

"What?" Hartas said. "What is it?"

"All right!" Michael shouted. "It's working! Stand still, let me mark it." He scratched a new pencil mark on the wall, one inch higher than the original mark.

"I grew?" Hartas asked in disbelief.

"One inch," Michael confirmed. "You are now three feet, seven inches tall!"

To keep his secret from his mother and brother, Hartas began to lower the hems in his trousers. Within the next two weeks, he had grown another inch and a half.

"You know," he told Michael, "we're going to have to tell them. Mom is starting to suspect something. When I left this morning, she looked at me kind of funny. She knows something's up."

"You're right. Even Emily noticed that something was different. She was asking loaded questions last night."

That night, when Hartas got home, he called his mother and brother into the kitchen. Barbara Seal was visiting Tom, and Hartas asked her to stay and listen.

"I have something I need to tell you." They gave him their attention, wondering what his announcement could be. "Mom, how tall am I?" he asked.

Mrs. Glen looked perplexed. "Why, Hartas, I don't understand... well, you know how tall you are. What is this all about?"

"Please, Mom," he insisted. "Please answer the question."

She looked uncomfortably at Tom and Barbara, and then murmured her response: "Three foot, six."

"What Mom? I can't hear you." "Three foot, six," she said, louder.

"Three foot, six? Are you sure?"

"Of course, I'm sure," she said, her voice showing a trace of annoyance. "You've been three foot, six ever since..." She went no further.

"OK, take it easy, Mom; don't get upset. Would you do me a favor?" The woman nodded, her puzzlement showing. "Would you get your tape measure," he requested. She looked at him strangely, but did as he asked. When she returned, he said, "Tom, would you take the tape and measure my height?" Tom opened his mouth to protest, but Hartas cut him off: "Please."

Tom took the tape and held it next to his brother. Barbara knelt down to anchor the end, while Tom read the numbers. "Three foot... eight and a half!" he said in amazement.

"What?" his mother said. "Let me see that! Are you holding the end right, Barbara? How can this be? I don't understand."

As they stood in incredulous silence, Hartas related the whole story of how Michael had the idea to visit Dr. Whitstone, and about the treatments and the doctor's prediction that he could be over six feet tall. When he finally concluded, the listeners were awestruck. At first, they stared at him, and then, their initial shock dissipating, they began to bombard him with questions: How long would it take? Did it hurt? Why didn't he tell them sooner? Who else knew?

At the Grae residence, a similar scene had just taken place, as Michael broke the news to Emily and her parents.

"Well, this is marvelous news, Marbel," Mr. Grae said to his wife. "We should help them celebrate."

"Yes," she agreed. "It's still early enough. Let's go over there. I'll get some snack foods and iced tea."

As she disappeared into the kitchen, Emily went upstairs to find her shawl. What an unusual thing, she thought. First the news about Hartas, and now this: Never in her whole life could she remember her parents paying a social call on a poor family. I wonder if Michael told them his ocean liner story, too?

20

CAUSE TO CELEBRATE

A few minutes later, Michael and the Graes stood on Arla Glen's front porch. Oh, Gene," Mrs. Grae said, "we really should have telephoned first."

"Well, we're here now, so we might as well go in," he said, knocking lightly on the door.

"Yes," she agreed, "But still, it's so rude."

Mrs. Glen opened the door, and seeing them, her eyes widened in surprise. "Marbel! Gene! Why... come in. Emily, how are you? Michael, good to see you."

"Oh, Arla," Mrs. Grae said as they filed in, "I'm so sorry for barging in this way. We should have called first."

"Nonsense," she said. "Our door is always open for you. Let me take your things."

"We just heard the good news," Mrs. Grae continued, "and wanted to help you celebrate. Is Hartas here?"

"He's in his room. I'll call him," she said. As she started toward the hallway, she continued, "Tom just left to walk Barbara home. He should be back any minute." From down the hall, they heard her knock and say, "Hartas? You've got company." A moment later, she returned. "He'll be right out. Please sit down. Make yourselves at home."

"We brought some cookies and things, Mrs. Glen," Emily said, handing the package of food and jug of tea to her.

"How thoughtful of you," she said, taking the food. "I'll get some glasses and plates."

"Let me help you, Arla," volunteered Mrs. Grae.

As the two went to the kitchen, Hartas came into the living room. "Well, hi," he said. "What's the occasion?"

"You are, silly," Emily answered. "Congratulations!"

"Yes, congratulations," echoed her father. "Sit down and tell us all about it."

"It's really good to see you again, Marbel," Mrs. Glen said, as she reached into her cupboard for some napkins. "It's been a long time."

"Too long, Arla," Mrs. Grae said. "What happened to us? How did we drift so far apart? We were best friends."

"That was a long time ago," Mrs. Glen pointed out. "That was high school. Afterwards, well, we just went separate ways. I married a garbage man and you married a business man."

Mrs. Grae laughed. "It sounds funny the way you put it. Remember the fun we had? We wasted our entire junior year chasing Jim Okun."

"Yes," Mrs. Glen said. "Wasted is right: He only had eyes for Marta. It seems so long ago. Now Jim and Marta have both passed away. He was only a year older than we were. Remember the time you dared me to ask him to a dance?"

"Yes, and you did!" Mrs. Grae said. "I couldn't believe you had the nerve to do it."

"Of course, he said no," Arla Glen continued. "He took Marta. How I envied her! And all that time, John Glen was trying to get me to go out with him. I wouldn't give him the time of day, but he never gave up. I couldn't discourage him, so I married him."

Both women laughed and then became silent. "Arla, is it too late to turn back the clock? I never had a friend who was closer to me than you were. Can't it be that way again?"

"I don't know, Marbel. But I'd sure like to try."

"I know!" Mrs. Grae said suddenly. With a hint of deviltry in her eyes, she said, "I have our old yearbook. Unless you come over for lunch tomorrow, I'm going to cut out all your pictures and sell them to Mrs. Bolan to use in the newspaper!"

Arla Glen began to laugh, and said, "You wouldn't dare! If you even think of doing something like that, Marbel Wilson Grae, I'm going to march right in there and tell your husband what you used to call him back in high school!"

"Arla! Don't you dare! He'd divorce me! Or murder me! Or both!"

Arla took her friend's hand and they smiled at each other. Squeezing Arla's hand, Marbel said, "Come on, let's get these dishes in there. If we're gone too long, they'll send out a search party."

"Well," Mr. Grae said when his wife and Mrs. Glen returned. "Where have you two been?" Mrs. Grae started to say something, but as she opened her mouth, Mrs. Glen caught her eye. Gene Grae's nickname: They both thought of it and began to laugh. "I won't ask," Mr. Grae said.

By this time, Tom had returned, Barbara still with him. From her front porch, they had seen the Graes arrive, and, sensing a party, had come back.

The assemblage quickly split into two groups, both talking excitedly. Mr. Grae, Michael, Hartas and Tom were discussing the figurine shop. Arla, Marbel and Barbara were near hysterics talking about Mrs. Enore's new hat, and how it was so huge that no one could sit next to her in church. Emily had disappeared into the kitchen to use the phone. A short while she reappeared and sat quietly as her mother told Mrs. Glen and Barbara about Ms. Shea's last visit, when she tried to hit Michael with her cane.

The two groups continued to chatter for about twenty minutes, when they were interrupted by a timid knock at the door. "Now, who could that be, I wonder?" said Arla Glen, as the conversants paused.

Emily stood, and, addressing Mrs. Glen, said, "Um, it's Alan. I asked him to come over. I hope you don't mind. I should have asked..."

"Not at all, dear," the woman said. "By all means, let him in."

Emily opened the door to admit Alan, who was looking very nervous. "Come in," she said. "And for heaven's sake, relax." Turning to the others, she said, "Since we were already celebrating some good news, Alan and I thought we'd add a little more." To Hartas she added, "You don't mind if we borrow the spotlight for a minute, do you?"

"Go ahead," he responded, laughing.

She took Alan's hand and announced, "Alan has asked me to marry him."

Dead silence. Then Mrs. Glen spoke: "Tom, be a dear and fetch the smelling salts."

"What for?" he questioned.

"Mrs. Grae is going to faint."

The room responded with roars of laughter. Soon everyone was hugging Emily and Alan. Mrs. Grae didn't faint, but she did cry a lot. She kept dabbing at her eyes with her handkerchief and saying, "Our baby... our baby" to her husband. As for Mr. Grae, he was grinning from ear to ear. His daughter: a bride! Never before had he seen her so happy. Tonight, she was twice as beautiful as she had ever been. Just like Marbel, the night they announced to her parents... He put his arms around his wife. "Look at her, Marbel." he said, his voice filled with awe. "She's grown up. She's a woman. And such a beautiful woman.

She looks so very much like you. We have a lot to be thankful for."

Marbel sniffed, nodded, and wiped her tears again. How quickly they've grown, she thought. It seemed just yesterday she was yelling at Alan for teasing Emily on their way to school. But look at him, she thought, so tall, so handsome, like his father. As she thought of Jim Okun, her eyes met Arla's, and she knew they were sharing the same thought.

21

REVELATION

"Well," said Hartas, as he came out of the store's back room, "it's finally finished. You want to take a loo..." He stopped halfway through the word, and Michael turned to look at him. Hartas' face expressed his confusion. What was wrong? he wondered. His voice had jumped at least an octave on that last word.

"That's it!" Michael shouted, his face alive with excitement.

"That's what?" Hartas asked, again in two octaves. He was clearly frightened. "What's wrong with my voice, Michael?"

"Don't you know?" Michael asked, still excited. "Don't you remember when this happened to Tom? You must know what it means!"

Hartas' mind quickly went back to his early teens. Tom was thirteen, Hartas a year older. Tom was afraid to talk out loud because his voice was changing. He started to grow taller, and within a year or two, he was shaving. But it never happened to Hartas. No voice change, no growing, no shaving. Nothing. Now, at twenty-seven years of age, he was entering puberty. As the impact of his realization hit home, he stood open-mouthed, daring for the first time to hope for the future. All the things he never even dreamed of were now possibilities.

How he used to envy Tom, going out on dates in high school, going steady with Barbara. But for Hartas, there had been only loneliness. "All the things I never had," he said aloud, more to himself than to Michael. "I'll be... I'll be like Tom, like Daddy. I'll be a man." He continued to dream out loud, and Michael listened quietly. "I might... I might even date someone. I might meet a man and even get married!"

The second he uttered these words, his heart skipped a beat and he froze in horror. What had he said? He hadn't meant to say that in front of Michael. In an instant, an entire conversation flooded his memory: Tom, in his senior year of high school, had done an essay on the history of sexual minorities. Some of the things he had learned were frightening.

"Did you know that some Outsiders have a real problem dealing with homosexuality?" he had asked Hartas.

"Why?" he had responded.

"I'm not sure," Tom said. "But for some reason, many Outsiders really hate homosexuals." It had only been an intellectual concept at the time. Neither had ever expected to meet an Outsider. But now, working so closely with an Outsider, Hartas had lived in fear of his friend finding out. And now, in one thoughtless moment, he had blurted it out. What would Michael do? Would he hate him? Hartas stood frozen, all color drained from his face. He couldn't even move his eyes, which were fixed on the store counter.

Michael's jaw hung open. Had he heard right? Did Hartas really say what he thought he said? Could Hartas Glen be...? And all this time, Michael had been so careful not to reveal his own secret. For what seemed an eternity, neither man moved or spoke. Finally Michael found his tongue: "What... what did you say?"

Hartas closed his eyes and drew in his breath. "I... I said... Michael... Michael, I'm gay..." He kept his eyes closed, and braced himself for whatever might happen next. Again there was a long silence.

"Hartas... you're gay?"

Without opening his eyes, Hartas nodded and drew in another deep breath, and held it.

"I can't believe it," Michael said.

Slowly, Hartas opened his eyes and looked up at Michael. His eyes, red from being held so tightly closed, now opened wide as he realized Michael was smiling. "You're not upset?" he asked.

Without answering, Michael threw his arms around Hartas. "Guess what?" he said.

One hour and many tears later, the two friends sat talking. "I don't understand," Michael said. "If being gay is so accepted Inside, how come I haven't met any gay people?" Hartas gave him a funny look. "You have," he said.

"I have? Who?"

"Well," Hartas began, "have you met Abby, at the cleaners?"

"Yeah," Michael said, nodding.

"Well, she's gay. And then there's Jon Zene at the bank. There are lots of us."

"And you use the word 'gay.' I thought that was an Outside invention."

"It is," Hartas said with a chuckle. "It became popular Inside in the mid 1970s."

"Why didn't anyone tell me about all this?" Michael asked. "I've been going crazy trying to keep anyone from knowing."

"I guess no one said anything because, to us, being gay is... well, it just *is.* Some people have freckles, some people can sing, some are gay. It's just part of life."

"Does your mother know you're gay?"

"Of course," Hartas said. "She's known for years. Tom knows, too. It's no big deal."

"What was it you wanted to show me before?" Michael asked.

"Oh," Hartas said, "I almost forgot. It's Alan and Emily's wedding gift. I'll get it." He went into the back room and returned holding two foot-high statues. He placed one on the counter, a perfect replica of Alan Okun in a tuxedo. Alan's left hand was held out at his side. Next to it, Hartas put the other figure: A likeness of Emily in full wedding gown. Her right hand was extended at her side, and when the statues were placed side by side, their hands met.

"Oh, Hartas," Michael said with awe in his voice. "They're beautiful."

22

THE TWO MADE ONE

It had been five and a half months since Emily and Alan had announced their engagement. Since then, Tom Glen and Barbara Seal had also decided to marry. Hartas had grown to five feet, six inches.

The day of Emily's wedding, chaos reigned supreme at the Graes' house. Beginning at ten in the morning, the doorbell rang every few minutes. Each time, it was one or two young women, loaded down with arms full of clothing, who disappeared upstairs. Michael sat in the living room watching as people continued to go upstairs, but no one came back down.

Mr. Grae brought the flowers for the bridesmaids into the house about noon. "Aren't they ready yet?" he asked Michael. As Michael shook his head, the older man said, "You'd think she could arrange to be on time just once." Going to the stairs, he called up, "Hey! Come on! It's time to go. Are you getting married or not?"

A few minutes passed, as Mr. Grae sat with Michael and waited. Five or six women made their way downstairs. "We'll see you at the Church," one called back as they hurried out the front door. The three bridesmaids were the next to come down. Barbara Seal, the maid of honor, wore a pale green gown with dark green velvet sleeves. The other two, Michelle Sanders and Tina Megan, wore similar gowns, but without the velvet. Michelle and Tina were a couple who owned a large farm on the eastern edge of Inside. Together, they produced a significant amount of the town's food supply.

"You all look terrific," Michael told them, as he handed each a small bouquet of white flowers tied with pale green ribbon. Barbara's bouquet had a dark green velvet ribbon on top of the pale one. Finally, Mrs. Grae came down with Emily on her arm. Emily wore a very old off-white gown with a long train. Her veil was of fine hand-worked lace, and trailed down to the floor. The front of the veil had tiny white flowers stitched into it. Mother and daughter paused at the foot of the stairs, as the two men held their breath in admiration.

Mr. Grae held out his arm to Emily. Smiling at her mother, she took her father's arm. "Daddy..." she whispered.

He handed her a large bouquet of white carnations with white ribbon and lace. "You are so beautiful," he said.

The bridesmaids led the way out the door, followed by Emily and her father. Michael offered his arm to Mrs. Grae. She wore a simple blue satin dress. It didn't quite match the color scheme of the wedding, but she insisted on wearing it. "I've dreamed of this day all my life," she had told her husband. "I always planned to wear blue, and so I shall." With a wink at Emily, she had added, "Indulge an old woman."

Outside the Church, Michael found Alan, his brother Shawn, who was the best man, and Hartas. As Michael pinned Alan's boutonniere to his lapel, he asked, "Nervous?"

"Yeah," he said. "Somebody wake me up when it's over." "Just pretend it's a rehearsal," Shawn suggested.

Alan wore a white tuxedo with a pale green shirt. His boutonniere was white. Shawn, Michael and Hartas wore pale green tuxes with white shirts and pale green carnations on their lapels. At the rehearsal, Michael had learned that Inside weddings were conducted quite differently from their Outside counterparts. Comparing the two, he decided he liked the Inside ceremony better.

At one o'clock, Hartas, Shawn, Michael, Barbara, Michelle and Tina gathered in the entrance hall of the Church. The pews were filled to capacity. The unseen organ began to play a classical piece unfamiliar to Michael. Hartas and Tina joined hands and slowly proceeded down the center aisle. When they reached the front of the church, they dropped hands, turned to face each other, bowed, and walked past each other to opposite sides of the Church. When they reached the outside edges of the front pews, they again turned to face each other. From the rear, Michael and Michelle entered and repeated the sequence. When Michael stood in front of Hartas and Michelle stood in front of Tina, Shawn and Barbara started down the aisle.

Once the attendants were in place at the front of the Church, Emily entered and proceeded down the aisle, with her father walking two steps behind. At the front, Emily placed her bouquet in front of the altar. From behind, her father gave her left hand to Shawn and her right hand to Barbara. He then turned around and faced the back of the church. Alan entered and walked down the aisle, followed by the Vicar's wife, representing the late Mrs. Okun. Upon reaching the front, Alan stood facing Mr. Grae. The two bowed to each other.

"What do you ask?" Mr. Grae questioned.

"The hand of your daughter, and her heart." Alan responded.

"What do you offer?" her father asked.

"My love," he answered.

"Emily," Mr. Grae asked, without turning around, "will you go with this man?"

"I will," she said.

To Alan, Mr. Grae said, "I give you my daughter." He then joined Mrs. Grae in the second pew. Alan stepped forward next to Emily, who turned around to face the Vicar's wife.

"What do you ask?" Mrs. Tey queried.

"The hand of your son, and his heart."

"What do you offer?" the woman asked.

"My love," Emily responded.

"Alan, will you go with this woman?"

"I will," he answered.

"I give you my son," Mrs. Tey said to Emily, and then sat across the aisle from the Graes.

A chime sounded. The Vicar entered from the side door, and the congregation rose to greet him. Shawn stood behind Alan and placed his hands on his shoulders. Barbara turned Emily around to the altar, picked up the bouquet and handed it to her. Then she stood behind her and placed her hands on her shoulders.

"An agreement has been made," Barbara said to the Vicar.

"An agreement has been made." Shawn echoed.

"Do you witness this?" the Vicar asked them.

"We do," they responded in unison.

"Then let it be done, the two made one," said Vicar Chelwith. "May the blessings of the living God be upon you both now and always. Will the parents step forward?" The Graes and Mrs. Tey stood behind Shawn and Barbara, who withdrew to the sides.

"I give you your daughter," the Vicar said to his wife.

Emily turned and stood with Mrs. Tey.

"I give you your son," he continued, and Alan turned and stood with Mr. and Mrs. Grae.

Mrs. Grae took Alan's hand and stretched it toward Emily, and Mrs. Tey did the same with Emily's hand. The bride and groom took each other's hands, faced each other, kissed, and turned to the congregation. Together, they walked down the aisle, followed by Shawn and Barbara, Michael and Michelle, Hartas and Tina, Mr. and Mrs. Grae, and the Vicar and Mrs. Tey.

23

CHANGES

Hartas stood six feet, two inches as best man at his brother's wedding. Tom and Barbara Glen rented a small house in the north part of town. Alan and Emily were living in the Okun family home at the corner of Main and Southton in the Village. Shawn, now 25, shared the house with them.

Michael and Hartas were doing a good business with their statues. Even though most families had two or three, the demand had not decreased. The two friends spent much of their free time together: dinners at the Druid House, picnics at Surday Park, visits to the Megan-Sanders Farm. And of course, they were invariably in demand at social affairs. Along with his new height, Hartas had a new self-respect. This same man, once despised for his annoying immaturity, had become a charming and sophisticated gentleman, noted for his humor and friendly manner. At Michael's suggestion, he had grown a moustache, creating a sensation among the traditionally clean-shaven Inside men. A sensation that became a trend: Soon, many of Inside's leading male citizens sported a hairy upper lip.

"Mom," Hartas said, "this house is too small. It's only one floor. We should have a two floor house."

"I could never leave this house, Hartas," said Mrs. Glen, looking up from the letter she was writing. "Your father's family built this house hundreds of years ago. It was the only thing he ever owned."

"I wouldn't ask you to leave, Mom," he said. "I didn't mean we needed a different house, just a bigger one. I've saved some money up, and I'd like to renovate the house and add a second story."

"Can that be done?" she asked.

"Sure. If you say it's OK, they could start work next week."

"Well," she said, "it's not really my decision. You're the eldest, so the house will eventually be yours. You decide."

"You'll love it, Mom. It'll be the best house in the east village." She just smiled and began to write again.

Marbel Grae and Arla Glen, inseparable friends, had established a custom of having lunch together on Wednesdays, and afterwards, dropping in uninvited on someone from their high school class. Survivors of the Class of '55 lived in terror of the 'tyrannical two,' as they became known. The two would show up unannounced, armed to the teeth with embarrassing yearbook pictures of their victims. As they left, they would threaten to give the pictures to Mrs. Bolan, unless their old school chum agreed to keep in touch.

In a matter of weeks, the Glen house had been transformed from a one-floor hovel in need of paint to a magnificent two and a half story Victorian marvel. The living room was doubled in size by knocking out the wall between it and the kitchen. A large brick fireplace adorned one wall. In place of the back hallway was a large, ornate staircase leading up to the bedrooms. Downstairs in the rear, where the two old bedrooms had been, a dining room and a modern kitchen took shape.

During the renovations, Arla Glen stayed with Tom and Barbara, who had explicit instructions not to let her near the house until it was finished. Hartas arranged for the completion to coincide with his mother's birthday. When the day arrived, they blindfolded her, and wouldn't let her look until she was standing outside the house. As they removed the blindfold, she looked up at the structure, blinking.

"This is our house?" she asked. "It looks like a new house."

"Only the upstairs is new," Hartas assured her. "Downstairs, the outside walls are original. Even the roof is the old one; they just raised it up. Come inside."

Arla opened the front door carefully, as though it belonged to someone else. Within the enlarged front room waited many of her friends and neighbors.

"Happy birthday, Arla! Welcome home!" they shouted. Marbel Grae took hold of Tom's arm. "Tom, be a dear and fetch the smelling salts," she said.

"Why?" he asked.

"Mrs. Glen is going to faint," she announced.

24

COURTSHIP

The months passed quickly. Emily Okun was eight months pregnant. It was early September. From her seat on her front porch, she was looking at the colors of the leaves on the trees across the street. As she sat in autumn reverie, Michael had come down the street unnoticed, and sat on the steps.

"The trees are pretty, aren't they?" he asked.

Startled, she looked down at him. "How long have you been there?"

"Just sat down," he said. "The trees are pretty. Fall is early this year."

"Thank God," she said. "Take my advice, Michael: Don't ever be pregnant in the summer."

"I'll try to remember that," he said in a mock-serious voice. "Tell me something, Mrs. Okun."

"What is it, Mr. London?"

"A couple of high school seniors came into the store yesterday. They were talking about a Harvest Party. What's a Harvest Party?"

"The Harvest Party is a very old custom," she began. "It goes all the way back to when most Insiders were farmers. Every year in early October, all the young couples have a party. It really doesn't have anything to do with the harvest anymore, but it does have social significance. Any couple who attends the party is more or less announcing that they are... what's that expression you use?... an item."

"Was there a Harvest Party last year? I don't remember hearing about it."

"Of course there was. But you never read the newspaper, and rarely poke your nose outside the store. How can you expect to know what's going on?" Her tone was teasing, and he responded by sticking out his tongue. "Anyway," she continued, "for future reference, the party is the first Friday in October, but tickets have to be bought by September 25th." Then, with a teasing voice, she added, "If you need a date, I know an available beagle."

He countered with, "May you be three weeks overdue in ninety degree heat!"

"I'd come over there and hit you," she said jokingly, "but it takes two people to get me out of this chair."

Hartas sat at his worktable in the rear of the store. In one hand he held the half-formed image of a man, in the other, a sharp tool. His hair and clothes were covered with wood shavings and sawdust. Michael stood unobserved in the doorway, watching him. He's so handsome, Michael thought. But it was more than physical beauty that he admired, much more. But what were the words for what he felt? He wasn't sure. He's so... Michael's mind searched for an adjective, but no suitable word was forthcoming. I like him, he said to himself. But not just that, I kind of need him. I depend on him. Almost like... Jeremy. Jeremy... he thought. How long since he had thought of Jeremy? In his mind, he tried to form a picture of Jeremy, but he couldn't. Each time he tried, the face was Hartas'. He felt annoyed with himself for not remembering Jeremy's face.

But it wasn't unusual for him to find Hartas in his thoughts these days. No matter what Michael thought of, the thought of Hartas was never far away. Why? he wondered. Something was obviously happening, but he wasn't quite sure what.

Hartas knew. Or at least, he thought he knew. He had known for some time. But he said nothing. He was too afraid. As the month of September drew to a close, Hartas began to feel very alone. Perhaps he had been wrong. Maybe he had just imagined the whole thing. After all, who was he, Hartas Glen, to think he deserved...

"Emily, can we talk?"

"Sure, Hartas," answered the rather large Mrs. Okun from her porch chair. She had become something of a permanent fixture in her chair, spending several hours a day there.

"Well," he began, "you know the Harvest Party is coming up."

"Yes," she said, nodding.

"Well, what I was wondering, I mean,... well, does Michael know about the party?"

"Sure, he does," Emily said, "I told him all about it myself."

"Was... was he planning to go?" Hartas asked, trying to sound unconcerned.

"I don't really know," she said. "Why?"

"Oh, no reason," he said quickly.

As Hartas walked away, head down and hands in his pockets, Emily began to think. Could Hartas be... ? With Michael? I wonder... she thought, and smiled to herself.

September 25th came and went. Michael never said a word to Hartas about the Harvest Party. It's my own fault, Hartas thought. I had no right to think all these big thoughts. I can't blame Michael for my fantasies.

By the day of the party, Hartas had completely given up hope of any of his dreams coming true. It was about noon when

Michael came into the store. Hartas sat behind the counter, reading the newspaper. "Where have you been?" he asked as Michael took off his sweater.

"I was trying to get an appointment with the Seers," he said, "but they're unavailable for comment. It doesn't matter. I think I've got my answer." Reaching through the curtained doorway, he threw his sweater onto a table in the back room. "By the way," he added, "Harvest Party's tonight."

Hartas felt a pang as he heard the words. Stinging tears filled his eyes, and he concentrated hard on the newspaper to keep them from falling. "Oh?" he said, with a valiant attempt at disinterest.

"Yeah," Michael said. "Do you know what it means if a couple goes to the Harvest Party?"

A tear fell onto the paper, and Hartas prayed that Michael hadn't noticed. "Yes," he said, cupping his hands around his eyes, so Michael couldn't see them. Why is he doing this to me? Hartas thought.

"Would you go with me to the party, Hartas?" Michael asked.

Hartas felt his heart skip a beat. The tears flowed freely now, and he was powerless to stop them. "Oh, Michael," he said, "we can't. We don't have tickets."

"Yes, we do," Michael said, reaching into his hip pocket and producing two red slips of paper. "I bought these a couple of weeks ago. But before I asked you, there was something I needed to be sure of. And I am sure now." He took Hartas' hands in his own. Hartas' tears still streamed down his cheeks as he looked into his friend's eyes. "Hartas," he said, "I love you."

25

THE HARVEST PARTY, A NEW ARRIVAL, AND THE QUESTION

The Harvest Party was held at the auditorium on the north side of the village. Mrs. Enore, as the acknowledged head of Inside society, traditionally took care of the arrangements. And of course, Mrs. Bolan always helped. "After all," she maintained, "if there are any announcements to be made, it stands to reason they should be made in my column."

By five o'clock, the hall was decorated with wheat, corn, hay, pumpkins, and other traditional symbols of the harvest. "How many couples this year, Celeste?" asked Mrs. Bolan, as they finished setting tables.

"Melfina said thirty. An even number."

"Hmm," Mrs. Bolan said, wondering what significance her friend attached to an even number of couples.

Six-thirty arrived, and Hildegarde Bolan was feeling very discouraged. Of the twenty-six couples already present, only three were "new" couples. All the others had attended last year: old news. And the three new couples were no surprise to

Mrs. Bolan. She was so much hoping for some exciting news to report. But so far, nothing.

Michael and Hartas were running late. At six-fifteen, they were still at the Glen's house. Mrs. Glen was in her glory, playing 'mother hen.' Not until both men were immaculate would she allow them to leave. As they stepped off the porch, Michael glanced backwards. Arla was smiling, and this time there was no doubt about it: she did have tears in her eyes.

As the two men entered the auditorium, all eyes fastened upon them. Certainly they had been seen together many times, but this was different; this *meant* something: Michael and Hartas were a couple.

Mrs. Bolan was writing excitedly in her notebook. This was news! Suddenly she stopped writing. This can't wait, she thought. Rising, she strode across the room to a telephone. From that moment on, the phone lines buzzed the news across town. It was many hours later before the switchboard operator was able to take a break.

The party ended just after ten. Outside the auditorium, another piece of news was making the rounds. An excited buzz passed along the word that Emily Okun was in labor. Hartas and Michael raced down Main Street to the hospital. Entering the lobby, they nearly knocked over the evening charge nurse.

"OK, boys," she said, "where's the fire?"

"We're here to see Emily," Hartas blurted out.

"Waiting room," she said, releasing them and pointing down a corridor. In the waiting room, they found Mr. and Mrs. Grae and Shawn Okun.

"She's still in labor," Mr. Grae told them. "She's having a rough time. Alan is with her."

For about four hours they waited with no word. Then Alan came into the room, looking pale and shaken. The group stared at him, and Michael felt a wave of panic. Oh, God, he thought, don't let anything be wrong.

At last Alan spoke. "It's a girl," he said, and started to cry. "It's a girl and she's beautiful."

"What about Emily?" Mrs. Grae demanded.

"She's fine," Alan said, still crying. "She fell asleep before she even saw the baby."

Named after her late paternal grandmother, Marta Okun weighed just six pounds. It had been a difficult delivery, but both mother and daughter emerged victorious.

Michael stood before the Seers. They were discussing his Seghva. "Inside has been really good for me," he told them.

"And you have been good for Inside," Harmor said.

"How?" he asked.

"Look at the valuable lessons you've taught Emily. That was wonderful. And look what you've done for Hartas! That was a problem no Insider could solve. You changed his whole life."

"Then, have I found my destiny?" Michael asked.

"You're finding it," Harmor said. "There is still one more thing to be done. You know what that is."

That night, Michael borrowed Alan's slahm, and He and Hartas drove to Surday Park. It was a cool, clear night, and the moon shone brightly. The two found a bench near the stream, and for a long time sat quietly. Hartas put his arm around Michael and held him close.

"Hartas," Michael said, "I need to ask you a question. Will... will you marry me?"

"Yes," Hartas whispered.

Far into the night, they sat by the stream, sometimes laughing, sometimes crying. Michael thought of Jeremy, and somehow knew that he would have approved.

26

A DREAM

It was daybreak before Hartas and Michael left the park. There was no reason to hurry; Alan wouldn't be needing his slahm. Like his wife, he worked at the bank. It was a very short walk to work, although a lonelier one, now that Emily was on maternity leave.

Michael yawned as he started the slahm. The once mysterious vehicle was now second nature to him. He still didn't know what made it run. The Seers said there was no English word for its energy source. But driving one was simplicity itself: one lever controlled everything.

"Tired?" he asked Hartas as they drove back to the village.

"Yeah," he answered. "Do you think it would be OK to leave the store closed this morning?"

"I think so," Michael said. "I'm too tired to concentrate on anything."

Dropping Hartas off at home, Michael parked the slahm outside the Okun's house. It's only six o'clock, he thought, glancing across the Green to the Town Hall clock. The Graes wouldn't be up yet. Leaving a note asking them not to call him for breakfast, he went upstairs to his room. He was asleep before his head hit the pillow.

Michael found himself in the Hall of Seer's waiting room. He couldn't seem to focus his eyes, and he realized he was dreaming. Before him was the picture of young Seer Marcus. In his ears were the words of one of the Seer's poems:

Slowly spinning, slowly down
Slower, slower
Till we can see
But there is time
Hated time
And will not set me free
Slowly dying, slowly down
Makes a prisoner of me

As the words died away, Michael realized that the picture itself had spoken them. Seer Marcus was moving and speaking, like a two-dimensional television image.

"Not very good poetry, was it Michael?" the picture asked.

"It wasn't bad," Michael answered, as if speaking to a picture were something he did every day.

"No matter," the young Seer went on. "It really did sound better in Fortu. But come with me now. Someone is waiting to talk with you."

Michael was instantly at the Seer's side. There were in a white place that had no discernable boundaries.

"Where are we?" Michael asked him.

"You know," Marcus told him. "The place is of your own design."

Just then, a third person appeared. It was Jeremy, dressed in the suit in which he had been buried. Michael was not surprised to see him.

"Hello, Michael," Jeremy said.

"Jeremy, I still love you," Michael answered. He was reaching out for Jeremy, but couldn't seem to touch him. "I still love you. You know that, don't you?"

"Yes, Michael, I know."

"Why can't I touch you?"

Jeremy responded with words from Marcus' poem:

"Farther moving, farther away

Far, far

Till none may touch

There is death

Intangible death

I have been set free

Brighter living, brighter far

Brighter than the brightest star."

"Do you know about Hartas?" Michael asked him.

Jeremy smiled. "I knew you would find someone. Do you love him?"

"Yes."

"Then I am happy."

"But what about you?" Michael demanded, his eyes brimming with tears.

"You'll think of me from time to time." As Jeremy spoke, his image seemed to fade. "And when you do," he continued, "I won't be far." He was gone.

"Jeremy!" Michael called. "Jeremy!"

"I won't be far," came the distant reply.

"I still love you, Jeremy. I still love you."

"I won't be far." It was just a whisper.

"Recite with me," Marcus said. As they began the poem, Michael found that he somehow knew the words. Together they spoke:

"I have been set free

Brighter living, brighter far

Brighter than the brightest star."

Michael awoke as they finished the poem. As his eyes tried to adjust to the light, he heard the distant voice of the Seer: "It really was better in Fortu."

What a beautiful day, he thought, as he dressed and shaved. He moved quickly, excitement bubbling inside him. It was already two in the afternoon. He flew down the stairs, waltzed a surprised Mrs. Grae around the living room, kissed her cheek, and rushed out the front door, yelling, "It's a beautiful day!"

Moments later, he pounded on the Glen's front door. Arla Glen rushed to open it, wondering who could be knocking with such urgency. With a huge bear-hug, he lifted her off the floor, whirled her around, and asked, "Hartas up yet?" She shook her head, pointing upstairs, too taken aback to respond verbally. Michael raced up the stairs and into Hartas' room. "Get up, lazybones!" he shouted at the completely blanketed form in the bed.

"I died," the blanket moaned groggily. "Go away."

"Come on," Michael insisted, shaking Hartas' shoulder. "Wake up."

"Have you no respect for the dead?" the sleeper demanded. "I was up all night with some lunatic in the park. I need to sleep!"

"You've slept enough," Michael announced. "If you don't get up now, I'll go tell Mrs. Bolan all your family's secrets."

"We have no family secrets," Hartas pointed out, still buried under the covers.

"Then I'll make some up. Come on, we've got plans to make."

"Planning a wedding isn't easy," Michael said.

"No, it isn't," Hartas agreed. "But it would be easier if you'd pay attention."

The two sat across from each other at a table in the back of the store. Hartas was writing on a notepad. "OK," he said, "we've got the date, the attendants, the flowers. Now we need to arrange for the reception. Any ideas?"

"Yeah," Michael said. "Mrs. Enore."

"Huh? Mrs. Enore?"

"Mrs. Enore," he repeated. "If anyone can plan a party, she can. I'm sure she'll do it."

"OK," Hartas agreed, writing down Mrs. Enore's name. "Now we need to get the license at the Town Hall, and talk to Vicar Chelwith."

Once the news was broken to the Graes and Mrs. Glen, they publicly announced the wedding. The article in the paper began with the notice:

London-Glen Engagement Announced

Mr. and Mrs. Gene Grae of Main Street and Mrs. Arla Glen of Alton Street take great pleasure in announcing the engagement of Mr. Michael London to Mr. Hartas Glen. An April wedding is planned.

27

REQUIEM FOR A SEER

It was the day after Christmas. Michael came downstairs at seven-thirty for breakfast, only to find the dining room empty. Mr. Grae, his face ashen, met him in the living room. "Put on your suit," he said quietly. "We have to go to the church. Melfina has died." Numbly, Michael obeyed.

At eight-thirty, Michael and the Graes left the house. Slahm buses were bringing loads of people from outside the village, all dressed in somber colors. Many wept. By nine o'clock, all of Inside stood outside the church. The steeple bell tolled seventy-eight times, the age of the departed Seer. When the bell stood silent, the church doors opened, and Harmor and Telesina emerged, both wearing black robes. Behind them stood an old woman. She was portly, and wore a black gown and veil. To Michael, she looked like Queen Victoria in mourning for her husband.

The woman stepped in front of the Seers. "I am Celia Telona," she said in a clear, strong voice, "wife of Seer Melfina. Behold, my husband is dead. Who will see for us now?"

A rather thin teenaged girl with long red braids, robed in black, emerged from the church and answered, "I am Marie, daughter of Seer Melfina. I am the eldest. Behold, my father is dead. I see."

In unison, Harmor and Telesina announced, "Behold Seer Marie, daughter of Seer Melfina, son of Seer David, son of Seer Sheila, daughter of Seer Seelad, daughter of Seer Felora..." The genealogy went on as they traced Seer Marie's ancestors. The crowd stood silently while the names were spoken. For over forty minutes, the Seers recited. Although Michael was bored, he was intrigued by their ability to remember so many names.

"...son of Seer Sanek, daughter of the Old Ones."

"The Old Ones?" Michael whispered to Mr. Grae.

"The Druids," he whispered back.

At that moment, the purple-robed body of Melfina emerged from the church, lying on a black velvet bier, which, like a slahm, moved without wheels. Under its own power, the bier descended the front steps of the church and moved to the center of Main Street, where it slowly proceeded to the Hall of Seers. Harmor, Telesina and Marie followed behind. Next came the widow Celia Telona, followed by the Seers' families. After them came Vicar Chelwith, and finally, all the people of Inside joined the slow procession.

The door of the Hall of Seers opened of its own accord to admit the body of Melfina. The Seers and their families entered the Hall and the door closed behind them. Vicar Chelwith led the people in a prayer for Melfina's family. As the crowd began to disperse, he reminded them, "Remember, everyone, all non-essential businesses must remain closed today. Food stores are open; medical and telephone services are uninterrupted."

"Where will he be buried?" Michael asked the Graes when they returned home.

"Buried?" Mr. Grae asked, not comprehending.

"Cremated?" Michael suggested.

"Cremated?" The older man repeated, still not understanding.

"Well, what do you do with dead people?" Michael asked.

"They go," Mrs. Grae said.

"Go?" Michael asked. "Go where?"

"Where?" she echoed. "They just go. Haven't you ever been to a going?"

He shook his head. Mr. Grae explained, "The bodies of the dead are taken to the Place of Going. It's a special room at the Hall of Seers. They are left there to go. It takes only a moment. Then the earth reclaims her own."

"I don't understand," Michael said.

"Well," Mr. Grae said, "when an animal dies, it eventually turns to dust. We also turn to dust. But in the Place of Going, it happens instantly."

"And what happens to the dust?" Michael asked.

"It's thrown to the wind. The wind carries it to the ground, and so the dust returns to the earth."

For a while they sat in silence. At length, Mrs. Grae asked Michael, "Outsiders actually bury their dead in the ground?" The whole notion was, to her, unthinkable, and she and her husband exchanged horrified looks.

28

WEDDING

Michael and Hartas were united in marriage by Vicar Chelwith. The ceremony was formal and quiet; the guests were limited to family and a few close friends. The reception, in contrast, was anything but quiet.

"This is an historic event," Mrs. Enore had pointed out the day she was asked to coordinate the celebration. "This is the only time an Insider has married an Outsider." No one realized it at the time, but what she was really saying was 'the whole town must be invited.' And invited they were. They came by the slahm-load to fill the auditorium. It might have been utter chaos, had Mrs. Enore not taken control in her usual charming manner:

"Back, you cattle!" she instructed the crowd, which instinctively obeyed. "Sit down at once!" Again, the mob complied. Throughout the afternoon and into the evening, Mrs. Enore saw to it that everyone had a place, and stayed in it. Anyone attempting to approach the wedding party out of turn was rewarded with a withering look from her, and quickly retired to their appointed spot.

In spite of her overbearing manner, Michael and Hartas were grateful for her presence. With her insistence upon order, the business of greeting each of the guests was soon taken care of, and the people of Inside prepared to eat and dance the hours away. At evening's end, Mrs. Enore, not a hair out of place and still very much in control, dismissed the guests in turn, each according to the slahm bus they arrived on. As the last tired reveler was dispatched, Mrs. Enore turned to the exhausted wedding party and fixed them with a stare. "Unless one of you brings me home immediately," she began, "there is a good chance that I shall sleep on the floor." This display of humor was most uncharacteristic of her, but nevertheless was well received by those addressed. She was, of course, immediately taken home.

29

THE VISION

"I can't just sit here and let it happen!" Michael shouted. His face was red and angry as he paced the length and breadth of the living room. Arla and Hartas watched him from the sofa. Neither had ever seen him so angry, and they were genuinely worried about what he might do. "I can't just let it happen! I've got to do something!"

"What can you do?" Mrs. Glen asked timidly. "The Seers said..."

"Forget what the Seers said!" he exploded. "This is your grandchild we're talking about, Tom's son! For God's sake, he's only a week old! How can you just sit here and let him die?"

"Michael," she began, her voice choked with tears, "believe me, I understand. Don't you think I love that child? I'd give anything if I could change what must be. But it cannot be changed." This last was spoken with a finality and resolution that Michael could not comprehend.

"Well, I can't just sit here. I've got to do something. I'm going to the Seers. They've got to listen to me," he said as he stormed out of the house.

"Michael," began Arla Glen, starting to rise. Her son's hand on her arm stopped her.

"Let him go, Mom," he said as she sat down again. "The Seers are going to have to show him... the vision."

"Oh, no. Oh, no." She buried her face in her son's shoulder and wept silently. Hartas looked toward the door, and shuddered.

Michael pushed open the door of the Hall of Seers, and walked in. "I don't have an appointment, but I want to see them anyway."

"I know," replied the attendant. "You're expected. Go in."

Without hesitation, Michael entered the Hall of Audi-ences. Harmor sat behind the desk watching him. The other two Seers were not present. A chair had been placed in the center of the room, and Harmor pointed toward it. As Michael sat, the Seer rose and came around to the front of the desk.

"I'm not sure where to begin, Michael. Today you placed all of Inside in grave danger."

"What?" This was not at all what he expected the Seer to say. "What are you talking about?"

"Michael, that child is going to die. None of us is happy about that. In fact, all of Inside is already in mourning for him. But the child's death is confirmed Seghva. You know that, don't you?" Michael nodded. "You openly challenged the Seghva. No Insider has done that in well over a thousand years. By doing so, you jeopardized all of Inside."

"I still don't understand."

"I know." He paused before continuing. At length, he sighed loudly. "Michael, there is a vision that is shown to every Insider as he or she reaches the age of reason. It is a terrifying vision, a thing of great horror, and we had hoped you would be spared it. Now there is no choice. You have openly challenged Seghva, and you must be made to understand the danger, just as all Inside children are made to understand." He paused, and then added, "Michael, I'm sorry. But there's no other way. You must see this."

The room became dark. Michael could no longer see Harmor, but he heard his voice, as if he were a distance away. "We once told you how we were descended from the ancient Druids, the Old Ones. We told you of the Insides in Ireland, Scotland and England. We also told you that the French Druids died centuries ago, leaving no descendants. Although they left no descendants, they left something else: A vision. They left a vision that has become the birthright of every child born in every Inside. Today, the birthright will become yours. It is a bitter and unhappy birthright, but a necessary one. Once there was a French Inside..."

As the far-off voice of the Seer spoke, the room began to blur, and it seemed as though the chair were moving. Michael gripped the seat tightly as his chair spun in every direction, in defiance of gravity and logic. A brilliant light appeared before him, and he found that he was no longer sitting, but standing. He was in a small village. The houses were all small, white huts with roofs of straw. The streets were dirt. Directly before him was a larger hut with a sign over the door. The writing was unfamiliar to Michael, and yet, somehow, he was able to understand the words: Hall of Seers. The wooden door opened as he approached, and he went inside.

There were two people in the room. Light from an indeterminable source illuminated their purple robes, and Michael knew they were Seers. They seemed not to notice him as he entered.

One of the Seers, a man, was weeping. The other, a woman, was trying to comfort him. "What is it, Niam?" she asked. "What's wrong? Tell me."

"My wife," he replied.

"What about her? What is it?"

"A vision. Seghva," he said as he wept.

"Show me," she said.

The weeping Seer nodded, and held out his arm to the wall. A glowing image of a wagon loaded with hay filled the side of the room. It was pulled by a black horse, and a young woman with flowing red hair sat on the wagon, holding the reins. The wagon rolled through the small village, passing an open shop where a blacksmith was about to hammer a piece of metal into a tool. As he struck against the anvil, sparks flew in every direction and the sound echoed in the street. Frightened by the noise, the horse reared up, and the wagon began to overturn. The woman screamed as the wagon rolled on top of her. Then all was silent. The wall grew dark again.

"Oh, Niam," the female Seer said, "I'm so sorry. Did you confirm the Seghva?" He only nodded. "When will it be?" she asked.

"This afternoon," he said. "But I can't let it happen. I can't. She's my wife. I love her. I have to stop it!" He turned, and ran past Michael out of the Hall.

"Niam! Niam!" the other Seer called. "Don't! Don't do it!"

The room faded and began to spin. Michael found himself standing in another room. A woman sat weaving at a loom. He recognized her as the Seer's wife. As she wove, she sang an odd song. Strange words Michael had never heard filled the room. *"Uri'a kiu'a kiu'a. U'a, u'a mor ba yon,"* she sang, keeping time with the loom shuttle. *"U fahl kiu'a kiu'a. U'a, u'a nor ta fon."* The woman had a clear, strong voice, with a haunting quality to it. A chill ran down Michael's spine as she sang.

Just then, the door of the little house burst open, and the woman spun around at the sound. "Niam! What is it? Why are you crying?"

"Valér, you must not go out today! You must stay here! Promise me!"

"What is it, Niam? What's wrong? Why mustn't I go out? You must tell me!"

"It's ... it's nothing. Just don't go out. Please!" His voice trembled with emotion.

"You're hiding something from me. What is it?"

"Nothing. Please, Valér, just promise me you'll stay home today."

"No, not unless you are honest with me. Tell me why you want me to stay in the house."

Niam finally relented and told his wife of the vision he had seen. For a moment she said nothing. Then she asked, "Is it confirmed Seghva?" He nodded. "Then I *must* go. You know that. You know it must be that way."

"You are the only thing I care about, Valér. Nothing else matters to me. Please don't go out."

"How can you say nothing matters?!" the woman asked with shock in her voice. "You are a Seer. Everything Inside is has been placed in your hands. Our entire future! Would you risk all of it for one life?"

"I would," he answered solemnly.

"Well, I would not! You are no Seer and no friend of Inside. I will not harm the place and people I love to save my own life. I will go out."

As she spoke these words, she did not notice her husband taking down a length of rope that hung on the door. She turned to reach for a shawl when her husband grabbed her and began to tie her hands with the rope. "Forgive me, my love. But I cannot bear to lose you."

The room vanished, and Michael found himself standing outside the blacksmith's shop. From where he stood, he saw the smith take a piece of metal from the fire. He held it with tongs and raised his hammer to strike it. For a moment the scene froze, and the awful realization came over Michael that he was about to witness the results of Seghva defied.

The blacksmith's hammer struck the metal with force, and the crash echoed all over the village. The door of the Hall of Seers flew open of its own accord, and two robed women rushed out. Michael recognized one as the Seer who had tried to comfort Niam.

"Oh, no!" the other Seer cried. "No!"

"It's too late," replied the first. "It's done. He did it. Cursed be the name of Niam from this day forth. Preserve the vision and let it be shared to all Insiders forever." The two women faced each other, joined hands, and raised their arms over their heads.

The sky grew dark, and a strong wind began to blow. In the distance, thunder rumbled ominously. The wind seemed to carry voices speaking words that frightened Michael, though he understood none of them, save the word "Seghva."

"Tinat go forú Seghva!" A flash of lightning filled the sky, and the roof of the Hall of Seers began to burn.

"Fenba kinu o Seghva!" Screams filled the air as several of the small houses collapsed. Lightning began striking the village at random, igniting some of the other huts. Panic-stricken Insiders began to fill the streets, rushing about in every direction.

"Sint u fúa ne Seghva!" The ground began to shake, and those buildings that still remained began to fall. As the shaking increased, people began to stumble and were trampled by others. Through it all, the two Seers remained unmoved with their joined hands over their heads.

"Seit nym Niam olm go finat d'Seghva!" The earthquake intensified, and Michael lost his balance and fell to the ground. The main street of the village began to split, and a huge chasm was opened in the earth. As the opening grew wider, the outer edges of the village seemed to rise so that the earth sloped

toward the pit. The slant grew steeper, and men, women and children fell screaming into the chasm. Burning ruins tumbled in among them. Michael lay on his stomach and held to the trunk of a small tree. In the distance, he saw the two Seers, suspended above the earth's open mouth, still holding their arms in the air.

"Bi sit nía fahn go Seghva!" As the last of the Insiders slid into the pit, the screams died away. The remains of the village were lifted up on each side of the chasm, almost vertical. Every last piece of wood, every stone, every child's toy, every animal, all of Inside disappeared into the earth. All that remained were the two Seers in the air, and Michael hanging from the trunk of a tree. Slowly, the Seers began to descend into the chasm, never lowering their arms. In a moment, they, too, were gone. What had been the earth was now a wall. Across the chasm stood another wall that had been the other side of the village. Alone, Michael hung from the tree that jutted out of the now vertical earth.

"'S Seghva!" To Michael's horror, the two vertical faces of the earth began to move toward each other, closing the chasm. When they closed, he knew he would be crushed between them. He tried to call out to Harmor to help him, but when he opened his mouth, there was no sound. As the ground closed over him, everything became dark, and Michael screamed in silence.

For a long time, there was nothing. Then, suddenly, Michael felt something in his hands. Wood. The chair. He was sitting in the chair, tightly gripping the seat. Slowly, fearfully, he opened his eyes. The wall before him was ablaze with sunlight, reflecting on a field of green grass and wildflowers. He heard the voice of Harmor saying, "And all of the French Inside was gone. There was left not a trace of the village. All of them perished because one man defied Seghva. The vision was preserved by two Seers, and became the heritage of all Insiders. Now the heritage is yours."

The scene vanished and the Hall of Audiences was once more illuminated with its normal subdued lighting. Harmor was sitting behind the desk. "Michael, we don't always like the things that happen. Even when you were Outside, there were tragedies that could not be avoided. They just had to be accepted. Sometimes, the things that are Seghva frighten us, and sometimes they anger us. But they must be accepted. Seghva isn't a bad thing, Michael. In many ways, it protects us. The natural disasters Outsiders must live with are unheard of Inside. We have no earthquakes, no tornadoes or hurricanes, no random lightning strikes, no floods, famines or infestations. There are very few incurable ailments here. All of these protections are because of Seghva. It is more than just fancy fortune telling, a means of knowing the future. It is a plan, a design. It is a controlling destiny, a protective power. It isn't God, and we don't worship it. But it is inextricably bound to every Inside and every Insider. It protects us from detection by Outsiders, and provides us with everything we need to survive. It is Inside, and it is every Insider. We can no more live without it than we could without air. The French Seer Niam, may his name be accursed, thought he could alter Seghva. He paid the price for his error, and all of the French Inside paid with him. That mistake must never be made again. As painful as Seghva may sometimes be, it must never be defied. It must be accepted. Do you understand?"

Through all of this, Michael never released his grip on the chair. His face was pale and fear shone in his eyes. He nodded to answer the Seer's question. He understood. As long as he lived, he would never forget the screams of the French Insiders as they fell into the earth, nor his own terror as he hung from the tree and the earth closed up on him. Nor could he forget the voices on the wind, or the sight of the two Seers suspended above the earth, preserving the vision so that no one would ever repeat the error of Niam. *'May his name be accursed',* his mind added as he thought the Seer's name. He understood, and he would never forget. He thought of Hartas. He thought of Mrs. Glen. He thought of Emily. All the people he had come to love so much, the Inside he had come to love as his home, all could have been lost because he wanted to defy a confirmed Seghva. The realization of what could have happened, and the thought of generations of European Insiders cursing his name, terrified him.

"I need to go home," he said. "I need to be with Hartas. May I... may I go?" The Seer smiled and nodded.

30

TWO YEARS LATER

Three robed figures sat behind their desk in the Hall of Seers. A rather animated discussion in Fortu was in progress, here rendered in English for reader convenience:

"Really, Harmor, you must be mad!" It was Telesina who made the accusation. Harmor opened his mouth to respond, but said nothing. He looked to Marie, hoping she would speak on his behalf, but she remained silent. Frustrated, he again looked to Telesina. Sighing loudly, Telesina said, "Well, we'll have to get confirmation, you know. Once before it was allowed. It sets a dangerous precedent."

"What are you saying?" Harmor demanded. "How can you argue with confirmed Seghva?" He looked from one to the other for some reply. Seeing none, he asked again, "How can you argue with it? You can't! Last time, Solana confirmed. Call her again. Go ahead, call Ireland."

Sighing again, Telesina conceded defeat: "Very well," he said. "Marie, would you call her?"

Smiling slightly, Marie nodded and closed her eyes. The two men watched her in silence. As Marie prepared to contact Seer Solana, a blue light surrounded her, its source indeterminate. "Solana," she called softly, "Solana." Before them on the dais, a column of sparks appeared. Shortly, it solidified, and formed the outline of a rather short, stout woman of advanced years. The blue light enlarged to include first the appearing woman, and then Harmor and Telesina.

Now fully formed, Seer Solana smiled. "Who summons?" she asked.

"North America," the three behind the desk responded in unison.

Again Solana smiled, "What is needed?" Again the answer came in unison: "Confirmation." Harmor rose and walked around to the woman's side. "What do you see, Harmor?" As she asked the question, she took both his hands in hers and closed her eyes tightly. For a few moments, they stood in silence, she nodding occasionally. The vision complete, she opened her eyes, released his hands, and spoke: "A most disturbing vision... totally unexpected, but definitely Seghva. Ireland confirms. Do you wish to contact England for further confirmation?"

Telesina shook his head. "No," he said, "unnecessary." He looked troubled, as did Marie.

"Understood," Solana said. "We're here if you need us."

"Thank you," Harmor said, smiling. Seer Solana and the blue aura vanished.

Harmor returned to his seat. For a long while, no one spoke. Each deep in thought, they sat motionless, staring at the desk. At last, Marie broke the silence. "Well, my Brothers, we have much to do." Both men nodded, neither looking up.

"Yes," Telesina agreed, "much."

31

THAT WHICH WAS LOST IS FOUND

It was evening. A young woman sat outside the bus station in Schenectady, NY. A light drizzle was falling and the woman knew she should move inside the building. But with the rain on her face, no one could tell she was crying. And so she sat in the rain and waited.

It was only a week ago, she thought. She had been in her mother's room at St. Clare's Hospital, looking out the window. *What a stupid place to put a cemetery,* she thought.

"It was there before the hospital was built," her mother said, perceiving her daughter's thought.

"Well, then, it was a dumb place to build a hospital," she insisted, not turning around.

"Laura," the old woman said. "Come sit down here next to me." Slowly, she turned away from the window and sat on the edge of the bed. "You don't have to be afraid, Laura. *I'm* not."

"Afraid of what, Mom? I'm not afraid."

"Of death. It will soon be time and I'll go. I'm not afraid."

"Don't talk like that, Mom. You're not going to die."

"Laura," she said kindly, "I'm a very old woman. I've lived a long and busy life. I'm tired. When death comes, I won't fight it."

Reaching down, Laura hugged her mother. For several minutes they held to each other. An old, old fear was gripping Laura. A memory from childhood: She, a four-year-old girl, asking if Daddy would come back from heaven in time for her birthday. When she finally realized Daddy wasn't coming back, a fear was born: What if Mommy went away, too? Another memory crept up: When she was six, she had become separated from her mother in a Manhattan subway station. The fear, born when her father died, had matured into a horrible demon named *'Alone.'* Her mother told her years later that they had only been separated in the subway for about two minutes, but Laura knew it was longer, much, much longer. For years, she had suppressed the demon, ignored it, till it was only a vague discomfort in her subconscious. Now, as her mother spoke of dying, the demon was released from its chains, and tormented her anew.

That night she slept in a chair in her mother's room. A nurse woke her at three-twenty a.m.: Mrs. Stevens had died quietly in her sleep. Left alone with her mother's body, she remembered the day Jeremy Tyler had died. Pushed out of his room, she and Michael London had clung to each other and cried like children. Michael and Jeremy had been like family to her. But now there was no one to cling to, no one to cry with. After Jeremy's death, Michael had vanished. She had tried many times to find him, to no avail. Now she was alone. Over the past few years, her mother had begged her to make some new friends: "Schenectady is full of nice young people," she used to say. But Laura preferred to stay home as much as possible. There was no one she could honestly point to as a friend. If only Michael...

Michael stood in the waiting room of the Hall of Seers. Before him was the picture of young Seer Marcus. But Michael's thoughts were not of Marcus or his poetry. He had a queasy feeling in the pit of his stomach. Why had he been summoned? Had he done something wrong? It had been more than two years since he last had a private audience with the Seers. Since that time, he and Hartas had opened a construction company, building new homes and renovating old ones. Hartas still carved figurines, which were sold as a sideline. They lived in the Glen family home with Hartas' mother.

The last two years had passed swiftly, and Michael felt very much a part of Inside. He rarely thought of the world Outside. But now his uneasy feeling somehow forced him to recall the past, as if Outside itself were trying to reach him. Why had the Seers sent for him? Surely they wouldn't ask him to leave, to return to his old life. Fear and doubt continued to gnaw at him, until at last he was called before the Seers.

The three sat behind their desk on the dais. Before them, Michael stood trembling, feeling much the same as he did the first time he stood there.

"Tell us why you're frightened, Michael." The request came from Marie. "Your thoughts are of Outside, are they not?"

"Yes," he admitted.

"Do you wish to return there?" she asked.

"No," he said. He felt his lower lip begin to quiver as tears formed in his eyes. "I really don't. Please don't send me back. I don't want to leave."

Quickly Marie came to his side. "No, no," she said, putting her arm around him. "You don't have to. You're part of us. We'd never ask you to leave."

"Then what?" he asked, trying to stop crying.

"We want you to tell us about Laura Stevens."

"Laura?" he asked. "But why?"

"Was she a friend of yours?"

"The best," he said. "We went everywhere together, the three of us..." A sharp twinge of pain hit him briefly as he thought of Jeremy. He continued, somewhat quieter, "She stayed right by me the night... the night Jeremy died."

"And what happened afterward?" Marie asked.

"Well, her mother was sick, so she moved back home to take care of her. It's funny; it all seems so long ago. By now, she's probably forgotten all about me."

"Let's sit down, Michael," Marie said, drawing him to the edge of the dais. As they sat, she continued, "Something unusual has happened. You know that Seers have visions. In fact, you remember that it was a vision that Harmor had that led to you coming here. With a vision, there are things that we, as Seers, must do to help people fulfill their Seghva. For example, we had to bring you Inside to fulfill yours. Once it has been determined that a vision is true Seghva, the Seers must do the things necessary to bring it to pass. Do you understand so far?" Michael nodded, and she continued, "Harmor has had another vision which has taken us quite by surprise. A Seer in Ireland has confirmed it as Seghva. We've taken some steps to bring it to pass, but we require your help to finish."

"My help?" he asked. "What can I do?"

"Let me tell you first what has happened," she said. "A few days ago, Laura's mother died. Laura had made no new friends in Schenectady, so she decided to return to Brooklyn. Last night she took a bus to New York City. She planned to take a hotel room for the night and look for work today. However, when her bus arrived in New York, we sent her a suggestion, which she accepted." She paused a moment, and then said, "Although she has no idea why, Laura is on her way to Tennessee."

Michael's mouth hung open. "You mean... she's coming here? *Inside?*"

"Yes," Marie answered, nodding. "It is her Seghva. I sense your approval. That pleases us greatly. She will need you, much as you needed Emily Okun when you first arrived. When the time comes, we'd like you to ride Outside to meet her... only as far as the barn. Will you do this?"

"Of course!" he said eagerly. "When?"

"Bryan Veller will contact you when it's time. She will need to stay at your home for a few months. Please extend our apologies to Mrs. Glen and Hartas for any inconvenience this may cause. Quite honestly, this has come as a surprise to all of us. But please go now. We three still have a great deal to do to prepare for her arrival."

32

PREPARATION

Within hours, all of Inside was a-buzz with activity. Street cleaning crews were out washing down the already immaculate streets. Business and home owners washed windows whether or not they needed washing. People bought new outfits; people had their hair done. Telephone Central was deluged with calls asking when the new Outsider would arrive. So many calls, in fact, that the manager was forced to take calls on the backup switchboard just to relieve some of the operator's burden.

Arla Glen completely emptied her spare bedroom of furniture, scrubbed the walls, shampooed the carpet, washed the curtains and then, not satisfied, repeated the entire process. She instructed Hartas to buy new linens for the bed, and seriously considered replacing the mattress, even though it was only two years old.

Mrs. Bolan and Mrs. Enore, each in her respective office in the newspaper building, pounded their typewriters mercilessly. They paused only long enough to phone Michael for more details about Laura. Mrs. Enore was interested in Laura's age, hair color, education, career interests, etc. Mrs. Bolan, on the other hand, wanted to know if Laura was running from the police, if she used drugs, if she was a bigamist, if there was insanity in her family, or if her family was ever forced to change their name to escape scandal. Of course, Michael answered 'no' to each question, and of course, Mrs. Bolan wrote what she wanted to, which was 'yes' to each question.

"Was there this much chaos when I came Inside?" Michael asked Emily. The two sat on the grass on the Village Green, while Marta, barefoot and droop-diapered, ran about trying to catch birds.

"More," Emily answered. "After all, you were our first Outsider. This place went nuts. And of course, half the village wanted to ride Outside to meet you. Most of those who went were sorry afterward."

"Why," Michael asked. "Was it because of me?"

"No," she said, shaking her head. "You'll be going out to get Laura. When you get back, I think you'll understand why they were sorry they went."

"Were you sorry?" he asked.

"Yes and no," she said. "I was glad you were here, but at the same time, I wish I hadn't gone Outside to get you. You'll understand when Laura comes."

"Do you think she'll like me?" Hartas asked.

"Of course she will," Michael answered. "Help me move this dresser." Hurricane Arla, having cleaned the spare bedroom twice, left it to Michael and Hartas to replace the heavy oak furniture.

"How do you know?" he asked, as he took one end of the dresser.

"I just know," Michael answered.

"Did she like Jeremy?" Hartas persisted.

"Yes she did, and she'll like you, too. So stop worrying and start working. If we don't get this room put back together, she'll have to sleep in the hallway, and then she won't be too thrilled with either of us!"

It was ten o'clock Monday morning. The phone in Michael's office rang. "Inside Construction. Michael London speaking. May I help you?"

"It's Bryan. The Seers called; it's time."

"I'm on my way," he said, hanging up the phone. "Hartas," he called, as he pulled on his sweater. "It's time to get Laura. Can you call your Mom and let her know?"

Bryan was already at the dock when Michael arrived. "Isn't anyone going with us?" he asked as he jumped into the slahm.

"No," Bryan answered. "No one wants to go." "Why not?"

"You'll know why soon enough," Bryan told him with a smile, as he too, jumped into the slahm.

33

LOST SHEEP

Laura got off the bus in McMinnville very confused and dazed. She took her suitcases and stood outside the terminal. For a long while she just stood, searching for some clue as to where she was, and more importantly, why she was there.

"Can I help you, my child?"

Laura turned to see an elderly nun standing by her side. "What?" she asked.

"You seem so lost. I wonder if I can help you," the Sister said.

"Oh, I'm OK, I guess," Laura responded, trying to hide her confusion. "What are those?" she asked, indicating some cards the nun was holding.

"Oh, these are for the orphans. They're holy cards the Bishop sent." Sister paused a moment, and then added impulsively, "Here, take one." She thrust one of the cards into Laura's hand.

"Thank you, Sister," Laura said. "Wait a minute," she added, reaching into her purse and pulling out a ten-dollar bill. "For the orphans," she said, handing the money to the nun.

"Thank you, my dear," the woman said, accepting the offering. "God bless you."

Laura looked down at the card in her hand. On the front was a picture of Jesus with a lamb on His shoulders. The reverse had just the words *"The Lost Sheep will be found in the South."* Not understanding, she looked up to ask what it meant. To her surprise, she was alone. The street was empty and the nun had disappeared without a trace. Looking at the mysterious card, she read the words again: *"The Lost Sheep will be found in the South,"* she said to herself. "In the south? ... In the south!" She grabbed her suitcases and went back inside the depot. "South," she said to the clerk. "I want the very next bus going south. I don't care what the destination is." Within the hour, she was on her way south, sitting on a bus whose destination she did not know.

Just south of Coalmont, the front left tire went flat. When all the passengers had gotten off to await repairs, Laura told the driver to get her suitcases. "This ain't a stop, Lady," he told her. "This bus don't stop in Coalmont."

"I don't care," she said. "I want my suitcases."

"Suit yerself," he said, and threw open the baggage compartment.

Laura, suitcases and holy card in hand, started to walk. A short distance from the bus, she stood at a rural intersection. Unsure of which way to go, she looked at her holy card: *"The Lost Sheep will be found in the East."* "In the *east?*" she said aloud. She turned to look down the road that went east. There, on the eastern horizon, she was sure she saw the nun waving to her. "In the east, then," she said, and began to walk toward the nun.

"I know I saw her," Laura said, perplexed, as she realized the nun was not there. She had walked about a quarter of a mile down the road, and now stood still again, unsure of what to do. Once more, it was her holy card that gave direction. It still maintained that the lost sheep would be found in the east, and so east she went.

Laura's watch said ten minutes to eleven. The sun shone brightly on the southbound dirt road her ever-changing holy card had pointed out to her. As she plodded along, her suitcases banging against her legs, she wondered if she were really being led, or was just losing her mind. Maybe she should turn back... This road probably led nowhere. It obviously hadn't been used in a long time, since there were no footprints or tire tracks in the dirt. She was on the verge of turning around, when a far away voice caught her attention.

"The Lost Sheep will soon be found!" Looking up, she saw the nun again, far down the road, waving to her. Quickening her pace, Laura continued down the road. This time the nun did not disappear, but continued to wave and urge her on, "Come! Hurry!"

An out of breath Laura reached the nun and sat exhausted on one of her suitcases. "It's all right, my child," the Sister said, placing her hand on Laura's shoulder. "The Sheep has been found. Look!" The woman pointed to an old barn, obviously long abandoned. Laura looked at the barn for a moment, and then turned back to ask the nun what she meant. But once again, the nun was gone, and Laura was alone. The holy card, too, had vanished.

Standing slowly, she turned her attention once again to the barn, and to the figure now standing beside it.

34

LAURA'S FIRST DAY:

MRS. BOLAN MEETS HER MATCH

"Laura!"

For a moment, Laura said nothing, frozen in amazement. Then, timidly, she spoke, "Michael? Michael, is it you?" He rushed out to meet her, and for a long time they stood embracing. She was afraid to let go; afraid he might vanish like the nun. The nun: where was she? Who was she? "Michael," she said, "there was a nun. She brought me here. Who was she?"

"I don't know," he answered. "We can ask the Seers later."

"The who?" she asked.

"It's a long story," he said. "Come with me now; I can't stay Outside anymore. It's giving me the creeps." He led the way behind the barn and deep into the woods, to the place where Bryan waited with the Slahm. "Now I know why no one wanted to go," He told Bryan. "I feel all torn up. Let's get back Inside. I don't ever want to go Outside again."

As Michael and Laura crossed the Green to the Hall of Seers, many passersby waved and called out words of welcome to Laura. The Seers spoke with her alone for about thirty minutes. As she emerged from the meeting, she appeared quite shaken. "Is all of that true?" she asked Michael as he led her out of the building.

"If the Seers said it, it's true," he replied. "They never lie. Get in," he said, indicating a small Slahm parked outside the Hall. "I'll show you where we live and introduce you to Hartas and his mom. And stop shaking. There's nothing to be afraid of. Trust me: You'll be happier here than you've ever been in your life."

"I'm not dressed right," she said, indicating her jeans. "All the women here are wearing long dresses."

"People here can wear what they want," he said as they drove toward home. "They wear Victorian clothes because they like them. You can wear dresses if you want, or your jeans, or both."

"Laura, I'm so pleased to meet you. I'm Arla Glen. Please come in." As she spoke, Mrs. Glen led Laura onto the porch and into the living room. Michael introduced Hartas, as Mrs. Glen propelled Laura into a chair. "Hartas, take her bags to her room," she ordered. "Michael, don't just stand there, get her a cup of tea." As both men left to obey her instructions, she sat opposite Laura, took her hand, and said, "Now, my dear, you mustn't be nervous. There's nothing to be afraid of here. We're your friends." As she spoke, the telephone rang, and she rose to answer it. "Excuse me," she said to Laura. "Hello?"

"Well?" demanded the female voice on the line.

"Emily!" Arla Glen said. "How nice to hear from you."

"Never mind that," Emily said. "Is she here? What does she look like? Where is she now?"

"Yes," said Mrs. Glen, "it's lovely weather. We hope to see you soon. So nice of you to call. Goodbye." She hung up. "That," she said, resuming her seat, "was Emily Okun. She's a very nice young lady, and very anxious to meet you. She asked questions about you," she added with a sly smile, "which I

totally ignored. She'll have to wait and meet you like everyone else."

Returning with her tea, Michael told Laura, "We have a lot
of catching up to do. We'll talk for a while, and then you'd
better take a nap, because I have a sneaking suspicion there's
going to be a party in your honor tonight."

It was two-thirty when Laura finally took her nap. Michael
had done his best to explain Inside society and how he had
been brought Inside. As he had expected, a party was being
planned. Mrs. Enore's maid Regina telephoned to invite them
to a formal gathering in Laura's honor. Once again, Mrs. Enore
had demonstrated that she did not understand the concept of
advance notice.

"Wake up," Michael said, gently shaking Laura.

"What is it?" she asked sitting up quickly.

"Unless you've got a formal gown squashed into one of
those suitcases, we've got to go rent something. Mrs. Enore is
having a formal gathering in your honor tonight."

"Mrs. Enore?" she asked, following him downstairs. "Another
long story," he said. "I'll explain on the way."

As they drove across the village to rent formal attire, he told
her about Celeste Enore and Hildegarde Bolan. "Here," he said,
handing her a newspaper clipping. "This is Mrs. Bolan's column
from today's paper. Go ahead and read it, but remember, it's
just a big joke to everybody but her. Nobody believes it. She's
dedicated the entire column to you. It's good, too. Even better
than the one she did on me."

Laura read the column he handed her:

Inside To Be Defiled Again

*For some unfathomable reason, our beloved Seers have once
again decided to permit an Outsider to move Inside. The new
intruder is Ms. Laura Stevens, a friend of our first Outsider,*

Mr. Michael London, now of Alton Street. It is our understand-
ing that Ms. Stevens is fleeing from the police under suspicion
of burglary to support her drug habit. She leaves behind two
husbands (that's right, two!) and a brother who is confined to a
hospital for the criminally insane. (The same hospital where at
least two of her uncles died.) We are told that the family name
was changed in 1924 to escape the shame of a scandal involving
Ms. Steven's grandfather, a feeble-minded waitress, and their
illegitimate child."

Laura's reaction was not the same as that of Michael when he first read Mrs. Bolan's column about him. For a moment, she said nothing. Then, she began to laugh. Within seconds, she was roaring with laughter. When finally able to speak, she sputtered, "This is rich! I have got to meet this woman!"

Her opportunity came a few hours later as they arrived at the home of Mrs. Enore. Regina made her customary announcement of each guest: "Mrs. Arla Glen, Mr. Hartas Glen, Mr. Michael London of Alton Street. The guest of honor, Ms. Laura Stevens of Outside."

"Mrs. Bolan is here. She'll act like she never wrote anything about you," Michael whispered.

"Don't bet on it," Laura whispered back. "I know how to deal with people like Mrs. Bolan."

As the guests introduced themselves, she listened carefully to each name, waiting for that one name: Hildegarde Bolan. And then, there she was, peering through her lorgnette.

"How... do you do?" she said extending her hand. "I am Hildegarde Bolan."

"Oh, Mrs. Bolan," Laura said quickly, taking her hand. "How nice to meet you. I've read your work. Such talent! But tell me," she went on, a wicked twinkle in her eye, "how is your brother? Is he out of jail yet? This is his fourth time, isn't it?

And have they found his wife yet? What about his girlfriend? Did she put up his bail or not?" Smiling sweetly, Laura waited for a reaction.

All over the room, jaws hung open in disbelief. Never before had anyone dared to give Hildegarde Bolan a taste of her own medicine. All eyes were on Mrs. Bolan, who in turn, looked at Mrs. Enore. "Celeste," she began, her voice betraying her deep shock and surprise, "did you hear...?"

"Oh, Hildy," Celeste Enore said, laughing. "Relax. You had it coming." Taking Laura's hand and shaking it, she said, "Young lady, I admire your courage." Turning to the still awestricken guests, she scolded, "Come now, look at you: a bunch of zombies. Close your mouths before you catch a fly! This is a party!" Raising her glass of punch, she continued, "I would like to propose a toast: To Inside's newest citizen, the very brave Ms. Laura Stevens."

35

FITTING IN

Laura's adjustment to Inside was far easier than Michael's had been, perhaps because she had him to help her. Within two months of her arrival, Laura was wearing Victorian garb and wore her hair the way most Inside ladies did. She was working full time as an art teacher at the Sinevor-Tesha High School. In her spare time, she could be found driving her new Slahm around town to visit friends.

Something else had changed for Laura, something she wasn't immediately aware of. It happened the moment she was met by Michael at the barn, as they held tightly to each other: *'Alone,'* that old demon from her childhood, had died. It was almost like a fairy tale, like Sleeping Beauty, where the kiss of a prince broke the evil spell. *'Alone'* thought his spell could not be broken. Laura's parents could not return from the dead. But finding Michael was, to her, every bit as miraculous. And it was enough to break the spell and banish the demon from her life forever.

"Going out?" Michael asked her one Friday night as she primped in a mirror by the front door.

"Mm-hmm," she assented, fussing with her hair.

"Why are you all dressed up?" he asked. "Are you and your friends going someplace special?"

Flashing an enigmatic smile, she answered, "I have a date."

"A what?" he said, jumping to his feet. "Did you say a date?"

"Mm-hmm," she said again, as she draped a shawl around her shoulders. "That's right." She opened the front door and, preparing to leave, said, "Shawn Okun is taking me to dinner at the Druid House." With a smile, she was gone.

"You should have seen Michael's face when I told him I had a date," Laura said.

Shawn sat across the table from her, looking uncomfortably at the prices on the menu. "I know what you mean," he said. "Alan had just about given up hope that I would ever date anyone. But there just didn't seem to be anyone worth dating before." Laura blushed, and Shawn did too.

The waiter interrupted with a message: "The owner has asked me to tell you that we have a very ancient tradition here, started about two years ago, whereby Outsiders don't have to pay for their first meal here. In other words, dinner is on the house tonight."

As they waited for their order, the two talked. The topics ranged from music to architecture to what makes a Slahm run. Even while they ate, they talked: Philosophy, history, literature. They found that they agreed on so many things. They seemed to share the same outlook on life, and to want the same things out of it. Laura was thrilled. It had been a long time since she'd met a man with whom she could communicate so well. Shawn, on the other hand, was mostly nervous. He'd had little experience with the opposite sex, and had no idea what type of impression he'd made. Did she like him, or did he bore her, the way the girls back in school always said he did?

When he drove her home, they sat in the Slahm for a long time just talking. Nothing serious this time, just idle chatter while he searched for the courage to ask her out again. "Laura," he began timidly, and then stopped, not sure how to ask.

"I know," she said. "I'd like to see you again, too. Can I call you?"

Too overjoyed to answer, he just hugged her, and she returned the gesture.

Later that night, as she sat correcting her students' homework in the dining room, Hartas came and sat with her. "Am I disturbing you?" he asked.

"No," she answered, "but what *is* disturbing me are these papers. Half of my students think Vincent Van Gogh lived Inside, and one person apparently thinks he was a Seer! Did you want to talk?"

"I was just curious..." he said. "What was Jeremy like?"

She smiled at the question. "Well," she began thoughtfully, "he looked a little like you, but just a little shorter. He was a redhead, too. He had a good sense of humor. He was fun to be with. But why do you ask?"

"I don't know," he answered. "Michael showed me his picture once, but he doesn't talk about him much."

"You would have liked him," she said. "He was a lot like you."

For a while, he sat quietly, watching her try to make sense of her students' work. At length, he spoke again. "Are you going out with Shawn again tomorrow night?"

"I'll be spending the evening at his house, but we can't go out," she answered, not looking up. "I promised to babysit Marta so Alan and Emily can take her parents to dinner. It's Mrs. Grae's birthday, I think. Shawn won't sit with Marta alone, because she walks all over him."

Again, there was silence, and Laura's face betrayed her surprise at some of the answers her class had written. "Oh, come on," she said as she read a particularly unusual response.

"Renoir invented the electric light? Who taught this class before I got here? A lunatic?"

"I guess I'd better let you get back to work," Hartas said, standing up.

"Sit!" she commanded, putting a final notation in red on the paper. Looking up, she said, "I wasn't born yesterday. You've obviously got something on your mind. Let's talk. What is it?"

"I'm not really sure," he said.

"Is it me?" she asked.

"No, not exactly," he answered, "But I'm just not sure. I like you a lot and I really admire you, too. But I feel like I hardly know you. I know you're busy with work and with your friends, and now with Shawn. Maybe I'm jealous of those things. Michael and I hardly see you anymore. I guess I expected that you'd be more dependent on us, but you're the most independent person I know. I admire that, and I think that at the same time, I'm jealous and I resent it." Through all of this, Laura listened quietly, resting her chin in her hand. When he finished, she said nothing, so he added, "Am I nuts?"

"Probably," she said, "but it's OK. I think I understand what you're saying. I guess I've been working so hard to put my own life in order, that I sort of forgot about you and Michael. You know, I don't have to be at Alan and Emily's until six. If you're free tomorrow afternoon, the three of us could drive around and terrorize the town. Maybe afterward we could have a picnic or something. What do you think?"

"Sounds great," he said, standing up. "I'll tell Michael."

36

STEPPING UP

"Mr. Lufe," Laura said, bursting into the principal's office unannounced. "Mr. Lufe, we have got to talk."

"Yes, Ms. Stevens," he replied patiently, gesturing toward a chair, which she ignored. "What is it?"

"Mr. Lufe, I've never seen such ignorance! Where did they get this garbage? Do you have any idea what I've been putting up with?"

"I'm afraid I don't even have any idea what we're talking about," he said in a soothing voice, hoping to calm her agitation.

"You don't know what we're talking about? You don't know what we're talking about? Let me give you some idea. This is just a small sample. In the five art classes I teach, I have six students who think Van Gogh was a Seer. I have two who think Mozart painted The Last Supper. One thinks Michelangelo was an axe-murderer, and two think the world is flat. One told me that Picasso was married to Mary Magdalene, and two said Impressionism is a rare disease. Shall I go on? There is more! Did you know that Joan of Arc painted the Mona Lisa? Or that Da Vinci wrote all of Beethoven's symphonies? Who knows what other nonsense is lodged in these people's brains?"

"I admit we have a problem," the principal said. "Our last art teacher was very old, and he was often confused. That's why we were so pleased when you applied for the position. But the ignorance you describe goes beyond the art department. This involves every teacher of every subject taught here. Obviously something needs to be done, and soon. Let me have a talk with the School Board, and I'll get back to you in a day or two. In the meantime, do the best you can."

By the end of the week, the School Board had named Laura 'head of faculty' for both the elementary and high schools. She continued to teach her five classes, but now she had some authority to decide what would be taught in all the other classes in both schools. Long a proponent of proper education, Laura welcomed the new position with its heavy responsibility, not to mention its sizable raise in pay.

"How is work going," Michael asked her one night, a few weeks after she assumed her new position.

"OK, I guess," she said. "It's slow going, but at least I convinced them the world is round. Apparently the former art teacher said it was flat, and a couple of students believed him. Would you believe I had to get a signed statement from the Seers before those two skeptics would believe I was telling them the truth?"

"I don't envy you your job," he said. "Not to change the subject, but I'm curious: Do you miss Outside?"

"Not a bit," she answered without hesitation. "My life is here. I left nothing out there. Everything I value is right here Inside. What about you?"

"This is my home," he said. "I could never live anywhere else. I don't miss Outside at all. But I did miss you. I'm sure glad you're here now."

"Not half as glad as I am," she said, taking his hand and squeezing it.

37

THE EARTH RECLAIMS HER OWN

"Emily, this is Laura. Is it a bad time to call?"

"No, I was just doing the dishes. It's Alan's turn to do them, but he was called back to the bank to fix the computer."

"Is it true?" Laura asked.

"That Alan's at the bank? Sure, it's true."

"You know that's not what I mean," protested Laura.

Laughing, Emily said, "Yes, it's true."

"How far along are you?" Laura asked.

"Well, the doctor said I'm two months, but I say I'm three, so who knows?"

"Have you told Alan yet?"

"Alan told *me.* That's one reason I say I'm three months. He told me three months ago that I was pregnant. I laughed at him. Two weeks later, I had reason to believe he was right. He knew Marta was coming before I did, too. It's weird."

It was Saturday morning. Arla Glen came downstairs still in her robe to answer the telephone. "It's only six o'clock," she grumbled as she made her way toward the insistent ringing. "Who could be calling so early on a Saturday?" she asked herself. "Hello," she said, trying to hide her annoyance. "What? Oh, Lord, when? ... Oh, I'm so sorry... I'll be there as soon as I can... I'm so sorry... I'll be right there." She hung up the phone and stood motionless, her hand still on the receiver.

"Who was it, Mom?" asked Hartas, coming down the stairs, he too in his robe. Seeing tears on her cheeks, he stopped halfway down. "Mom, what happened? What's wrong?"

Looking up at him, she answered, "Gene Grae is dead. Please, go wake up Michael and Laura, and call your brother and tell him. I've got to get dressed and go over there. Marbel needs me."

If at all possible, an Inside funeral is held the same day a person dies. By nine a.m., much of Inside was in mourning. Even nature seemed to mourn, as a fierce thunderstorm raged in the heavens. Rain fell heavily all morning. Outside the church, Michael found Emily in the crowd. She was dressed in black, and appeared dazed, as if her consciousness were not a part of the scene around her. "Emily," he said, putting out his arms.

"Michael," she cried, putting her arms around him and clinging tightly. "My Daddy's gone. My Daddy..." He said nothing, but held her tightly.

Marbel Grae emerged from the church, leaning heavily on her son-in-law Alan and Arla Glen. Shortly afterward, the bier upon which Gene Grae was laid emerged from the church, descended the steps, and moved slowly toward the Hall of Seers, all under its own power. Outside the Hall, the Seers waited in black robes. As the bier approached, they moved aside to admit it. Behind the body followed the widow, and then Emily, Alan and Marta. As the bereaved family entered the Hall, Mrs. Grae turned around and asked, "Where's Michael?"

Stepping out of the crowd, he weakly responded, "Here."

"You come in, too," she said.

The procession moved on: First the bier, then Mrs. Grae, then Emily, Alan and Marta, then Michael, and finally the Seers. The crowd remained outside where Vicar Chelwith spoke with them. The bier led the family down the hallway, past the Hall of Audiences, to a door labeled, 'The Place of Going.' The door opened of its own accord, and the bier moved to the front of the semi-darkened room. The family members stood against the back wall, while the Seers took their place behind the bier, their backs to the front wall. Harmor spoke, "You may pay your respects. Marbel?"

Mrs. Grae approached the body of her husband. She shook visibly as she took his hand. "Gene," she whispered as she wept, "you gave me the best years of my life. I don't know how I'll go on without you, but I know I'll never forget you. I love you." She stood weeping a few moments longer, and then returned to her place.

"Emily and Marta?" Harmor called.

Mother and daughter approached the bier. "Grandpa?" Marta asked her mother, who nodded in response. "Grandpa, get up!" the child ordered."

"Grandpa can't get up, honey," Emily said. And then, to her father she said, "Daddy... Daddy..." She said nothing more. Weeping, she picked up her daughter and returned to the back of the room.

"Alan?" said Harmor.

Alan took his place before the bier, and spoke quietly. "I promised you I'd take care of Emily. I kept that promise. I promise I'll take care of her Mom, too. You won't have to worry, Dad. I'll take care of..." His voice failed as he, too, wept. Returning to his wife and daughter, he placed his arm around his mother-in-law and held her close.

"Michael," called out Harmor.

Standing next to the body, Michael said, "Mr. Grae, ever since I came Inside, you've been like a father to me. I love you and I'll miss you."

All goodbyes said, the bereaved stood back against the wall again. The Seers, behind the bier, joined hands and called out in unison, "To the mercy of God we commit the soul of Gene Grae. Let the earth reclaim her own." For a split second there was a blinding flash of light, and then the body was gone. In its place remained only a fine, white dust. Harmor collected the dust in a small, gold dish, and the Seers led the family out. Outside the Hall, most of the crowd had gone, but a few remained to comfort the family. Together the Seers walked out into the street and threw the dust of Mr. Grae to the wind. In a few moments, all trace of it was gone, carried away by wind and rain.

38

LIFE GOES ON

After the death of her husband, Marbel Grae found it difficult to live alone. Many nights she couldn't sleep, and sat all night listening to the radio. For the first week, Arla Glen stayed with her, cooked her meals and cleaned her house. Together, Arla and Laura packed up Mr. Grae's clothes and brought them to the church for distribution among the needy.

One afternoon, Arla stopped at the bank to talk with Alan. "Something is going to have to be done for Marbel. Now that she's alone in that house, she's not sleeping, she forgets to eat; she just sits up all night listening to Barbra Streisand on the radio."

"What can we do?" he asked, his voice showing concern.

"Well," she went on, "Gene left the house to Marbel, with the understanding that it be given to Emily after Marbel is gone. If you would be willing, you and Emily could move in with her now. I know she'd be delighted to have you, and with a baby on the way, Emily could use some extra help with Marta."

"I have no objection," he said, "if Emily agrees. But what about my house? The Okuns have lived in that house for over two hundred and fifty years. I wouldn't want to sell it out of the family."

"Ooh!" she said, pinching his cheek in a motherly fashion. "You're cute, but you're dumb! Have you ever considered that you have a younger brother? He's an Okun, and he didn't inherit any house!"

"It makes sense," he admitted, rubbing his cheek where she had pinched too hard. "I'll talk to Emily tonight."

"It sounds like a good idea," Emily said that night over dinner. "But will my mother agree?"

"If she's approached right," Alan said. "Let me show you." Going to the phone, he dialed the number. "Mom? ... Hi, how are you doing? ... I'm fine... She's fine, too... Marta? Cute and spoiled, of course. Mom, we have a problem we were hoping you might be able to help us with. With the baby coming, Emily isn't sure she'll be able to manage both Marta and the new one. She's really going to have her hands full. We thought of a solution, but it's kind of an inconvenience for you. We're a little embarrassed to ask... Could we move in with you? ... Well, we thought we'd give this house to Shawn. He'll be needing one eventually... You don't mind? ... You're sure? ... Great. We really appreciate it. Thanks, Mom... We love you, too."

"She went for it?" Emily asked as he hung up the phone.

"Let me put it this way," he said. "Before she even hung up, she had already mentally redecorated the spare bedroom for a nursery, and had chosen the colors to repaint your old room for us... She's thrilled!"

"Wait a minute, Shawn," Laura said into the phone. "Let me get this straight. They gave you the house? ... For free? ... Just like that? Incredible! You should have a party... We can invite Tom and Barb, Michael and Hartas, Alan and Emily, Michelle and Tina... Who else?"

With her new household of people, Marbel Grae found herself with plenty to do. And the extra activity was just the therapy she needed: After a full day of Marta, she was ready to sleep. Every morning by seven o'clock, Marta was up, singing nursery rhymes to her dolls, and Emily, a far better cook than Alan, was making breakfast. "Mom," she would call upstairs, "I'm making breakfast. One egg or two?"

"Oh, I'm not hungry, dear. Don't make any for me."

Ignoring the unacceptable response, Emily repeated, "One egg or two?"

"None!" came the reply.

"One egg or two, Mom?"

"Oh, for heaven's sake, make it two, then!" Marbel would shout. After a couple of days of scenes like this, Marbel realized that she was going to eat three full meals a day, like it or not. Arla Glen made it a point to take her shopping at least once a week. It didn't take long before Marbel was back to her old self, she and Arla paying surprise visits to their old schoolmates.

39

AUTUMN SURPRISES

Autumn came early that year. By mid-August, the leaves had changed and were falling. Emily was grateful for the cooler weather, having once again suffered the heat of summer while pregnant.

It was a Thursday afternoon. Emily was returning from a doctor's appointment. Coming slowly into the house, she lowered herself gently onto the couch. A dazed expression was on her face.

"Emily," her mother said, coming downstairs. "Are you all right? What did Dr. Whitstone say?"

"Two," Emily answered, as if in a dream.

"Too?" Marbel echoed. "Too what?"

"Two," her daughter repeated, holding up two fingers. "Two... Two babies."

Marbel looked at her daughter for a moment, not comprehending. As the understanding began to dawn, she said, "Twins? You're going to have twins?"

Emily nodded. "Two," she said numbly. "Two babies."

The second week of September found Emily Okun in advanced pregnancy, large and uncomfortable. "It'll be over soon," Alan reassured her. "We'll wait a few years before the next one."

"What next one?" she asked in a threatening tone of voice.

At two-fifteen the next morning, Emily shook her husband. "Alan, wake up."

"Mmphffgrf," he replied.

"Alan," she insisted. "Wake up. It's time." Trying to roll over and jump up at the same time, Alan found himself deposited on the floor. "Are you quite awake, now?" his wife asked.

"I'll go call the doctor," he said, picking himself up.

"I did that," she said.

"Then I'll go tell Mom."

"I did that, too," she replied.

"I'll get the slahm out of the garage, then."

"I did that already," she said. "Why don't you just get dressed?" Picking up her suitcases, she opened the bedroom door. "Your clothes are on the chair," she said as she left the room.

Gene and James Okun were born at four thirty-five and four-forty a.m. respectively. They both weighed in at six pounds, two ounces. Named after their paternal grandfathers, the twins were identical in every respect, including volume. When the boys awoke for a two a.m. feeding, the neighborhood knew.

Laura and Shawn were sitting in the library, pretending to read a book on Plato. "Laura," Shawn began, "would you... do you want to... there's the..."

"The Harvest Party," she supplied. "I'd love to."

Shawn smiled. "That's what I love about you," he said. "You always know what I want to say."

The day before the party, Shawn went to talk to the Seers. "You know I've been dating Laura Stevens," he began. "That's what I want to ask you about. I'd like to... I want to ask her... I want to marry her."

The Seers exchanged smiles. "We have no objections, of course," said Telesina. "But there are some things you must know. As you are aware, she is an Outsider. As such, she is not of the same species as we. Without special help, the two of you would be unable to conceive a child."

"Are we that different?" Shawn asked.

"More than you imagine," the Seer answered. "But Dr. Whitstone has been preparing for this, and he should be able to help if you desire to have children."

Shawn and Laura didn't create quite the stir that Michael and Hartas did at their first Harvest Party. Scarcely an eyebrow was raised when they made their entrance, which was just fine with them.

40

A QUESTION IN THE NIGHT

Shawn and Laura were in the woods south of the village, not far from the stream. It was night, and the darkness was thick around them. Even thought it was too dark to see, they were not afraid. This was 'their' place; they came here often. They would sit and listen to the stream, or count the stars through the trees. Tonight, they lay on the ground together, side-by-side, listening to the leaves, the stream, an occasional owl. Entranced by the sounds of night, they lay in silence. As the night wore on, a light rain began to fall. Huddled together for warmth, they heard each other breathe.

"Laura," Shawn said quietly.

"Mm?" she answered.

"I want to... I mean... will... I want to ask... I don't know how to say it. You always know what I'm trying to say; can't you figure it out this time?"

"Of course," she said. "But I won't. I've waited all my life for this, so you're just going to have to find the words. Just relax, take a deep breath, and take your time."

He did as she suggested, inhaling deeply, exhaling, and making a conscious effort to relax. "I want to... to ask you... if you will... marry me." The words uttered, he closed his eyes, held his breath and waited.

"You know I will," she said.

"You... you will?" he asked, almost incredulously.

"Of course," she said. "I decided to marry you weeks ago, but I had to wait for you to ask. I thought about asking you, but I decided not to. That way, when you asked me, I'd know you felt the same way I do... I love you, Shawn Okun."

Putting his arms around her, Shawn kissed her, and whispered, "I love you, too, Laura Stevens."

41

PASSAGE OF TIME

It was a dark day in November. From early morning, the skies had threatened heavy rain. Laura looked out of the living room window onto Main Street. It was two years to the day since she had moved into the Okun family home.

Shawn was down in the south part of town washing windows for the Taravels. His was the only window washing service in town, and it did a good business among the wealthier Insiders. Now as the sky grew darker, Laura wished he would come home.

"Something is very wrong," she said aloud. "Something bad is going to happen." It wasn't Shawn she was worried about. If he had been in trouble, she would have known; she had a sense about those things. It was someone else. The first few drops of rain hit the windowpane, slid down, and were quickly replaced by others. A clap of thunder shook the house, and suddenly she knew. Picking up the phone, she dialed the number.

"Inside Constr.." began the voice.

"Hartas," she interrupted. "Get home. Something's wrong. I'll meet you there." She hung up the phone and raced out to her slahm, throwing a sweater around herself. It was raining hard now, and a constant rumble of thunder was heard in the sky.

As she pulled up in front of the Glen home, she was trembling, partly from cold and partly from fear. She ran up the walk and pounded on the door. Michael answered, his face ashen. From inside the house, she heard crying. "It's Mrs. Glen," he said as she entered. "A stroke, I think. Dr. Whitstone's on his way."

"Where's Hartas?" she asked, taking her wet sweater off.

"He's on the phone with Barbara."

Dr. Whitstone came in behind Laura. "Where is she?" he asked.

"Upstairs," Michael answered. "I'll show you." The two went upstairs, leaving Laura alone in the living room.

Shortly, a teary-eyed Hartas emerged from the kitchen. "Laura," he began. "Thank you. But how did you know?"

"I just knew," she said. "Sometimes I just know."

There was a knock at the door, and Hartas opened it. Vicar Chelwith, drenched through, came into the house. "I'm sorry I couldn't get here sooner. My wife has the slahm. Is your mother upstairs?" Hartas nodded, and the minister disappeared upstairs.

Laura and Hartas sat together and waited. Laura felt awkward, not knowing what to say, but in truth, Hartas was grateful for her company. About twenty minutes later, Michael, the Vicar and Dr. Whitstone came downstairs. Laura and Hartas stood quickly, and he asked, "Is she all right?"

"She's sleeping now," the doctor said, "but yes, she's going to be all right. I don't expect any complications. Bring her around to the office tomorrow, though. I'd like to run a few tests, just to be sure." He turned to leave, and then stopped. "Oh, Laura," he said, "I wonder if I might have a word with you?" The two went into the kitchen for a moment, and then returned. The doctor gave last minute instructions to Hartas, and then followed Vicar Chelwith out into the storm.

"What did the doctor want?" Michael asked Laura.

"He had some test results for me," she said with an enigmatic smile.

"Oh?" Michael said.

"Mm-hmm," she said nodding. "After six failures, we have a success." Both men looked at her with puzzled expressions. "I'm pregnant!" she blurted out.

Each time Dr. Whitstone had attempted his feat of genetic engineering, something had gone wrong. The first two times, the problem was Laura's biological clock, which had inexplicably triggered menstruation within hours of the fertilized egg being introduced into her womb. That problem was solved by the use of a drug that regulated her cycle. The next three attempts failed when the egg cell died shortly after implantation. The sixth attempt never even got that far: For some reason, the sperm cells refused to attempt fertilization. But the seventh time offered hope right from the start. The Insider chromosomes were implanted in the ovum without difficulty, and the cell was quickly fertilized. Following implantation, it was just a matter of time. The earliest pregnancy test available Inside is three weeks after fertilization. In Laura's case, test number seven was positive.

Arla Glen's tests showed no long-term effects from her stroke. Dr. Whitstone prescribed exercise, proper diet, and monthly checkups. He also warned that failure to follow these instructions could lead to another stroke, far more serious than the first. Mrs. Glen wasn't the best at following the instructions, so Laura and Marbel came to the rescue. Mrs. Grae called her friend every day to remind her to exercise. Often, they exercised together. Laura, on the other hand, with her uncanny ability to know things, made sure Mrs. Glen stuck to her diet. It was not uncommon for Mrs. Glen to get three word phone calls from Laura, the three words being, "Put that down!" These calls invariably coincided with Arla picking up some forbidden delicacy. Once, Laura called at three a.m. She had woken up out of a sound sleep and had known that Mrs. Glen was having a "midnight snack." She didn't pick up the phone though, until she reached for the bacon. Instantly, Laura was on the phone: "Put it back... the bacon... Don't try to con me, Arla Glen. I know what you're doing. How am I supposed to get a good night's sleep with you raiding the refrigerator? Now close the door and go back to bed."

42

MS. SHEA'S
INTERPLANETARY PEACE

"Inside Construction. Michael London speaking."

"It's Laura. Why isn't there a fire department?"

"What?"

"There's no fire department," she said. "I just realized it. Why not?"

"Have you ever seen a building burn?" he countered.

"No," she admitted.

"And you never will," he said. "There are no house fires Inside. The Seers have a lot of control over things like that. It has to do with Seghva."

"What else?" she asked.

"Well, let's see if I can remember: No earthquakes, tornadoes, hail or other natural disasters."

"What about sickness?" she asked. "Why do people still get sick?"

"Their power over sickness is limited," he answered, "but there are no major plagues. And they can't stop anyone from dying if it's their time to go."

"That's fascinating," she said. "I wonder if... Oh, Lord!"

"What is it?" he asked.

"You won't believe who's at my door," she answered. "Who?"

"Ms. Shea," she said, "and get this: She's holding a shovel!"

"You could pretend you're not home," he suggested.

"No," she said, "I can't. She's looking right at me through the window. I'll have to let her in."

"Have fun," he told her. "I'll call you later."

Hanging up the phone, Laura went to the door to admit the old woman. "Hello, Ms. Shea," she said. "How are you?"

"Just fine, dear. May I come in?"

"Of course. Would you like to leave your shovel by the door?"

"Oh, no," she said. "I need to keep it nearby." Leaning closer to Laura, she whispered, "This is no ordinary shovel. It's

a bubble-popping shovel. All of Inside is overrun by bubbles. I've been out popping them all morning. I just stopped by to warn you that some of them got away. May I have a cup of tea?"

"Sure," Laura said. "Come sit in the living room. I'll make the tea."

She returned a few moments later with the tea, and found Ms. Shea on the phone, arguing with someone. "What do you mean it isn't possible?" she demanded. "I've done it dozens of times. Don't you understand how important this is? We've only just signed a peace treaty with them. It's essential that we keep the lines of communications open... What? No phone lines to there? Well, I've never heard of such a thing!" She hung up and turned to Laura. "No phone lines to Mars," she said. "Have you ever heard anything so ridiculous? What kind of operator is she if she can't get me a line to Mars?"

For the next hour, Ms. Shea filled Laura in on all her recent activities, including how she had signed peace treaties with six of the planets in this solar system. Returning from the kitchen with a second pot of tea, Laura again found Ms. Shea on the phone. "What? Still no lines? Then I suggest you get out and string some! Impudent woman!" she exclaimed, hanging up the phone. "Well, Laura," she said, "I really should be going. At least three bubbles escaped. I have my work cut out for me."

"You know, Ms. Shea," Laura said as they started for the door, "it's too bad I didn't know you when I was Outside. I could have benefited a lot from someone like you."

The old woman stopped, and looked at Laura with a very serious expression. "Oh, no, my dear," she said. "I could never be like this Outside. They'd put me in a hospital and give me drugs to make me act like everyone else. I'd be so unhappy."

"Yes," Laura agreed, nodding thoughtfully. "You would be unhappy out there. I know I was. I'm glad I'm Inside now."

"So am I, dear," said Ms. Shea, patting her hand and turning to leave, shovel ready for bubble popping.

43

EPILOGUE

The three stood in front of the Hall of Seers, attired in their finest purples robes: Seer Telesina, Seer Marie, and Seer Thomas, son of the late Seer Harmor.

"It's hard to believe it's been ten years," said Telesina, pulling his robe tighter to shield himself from the cold night air.

"Yeah," agreed Thomas, "and you thought Dad was nuts when he told you it was gonna happen."

"Well, could you blame me?" the older man asked. "After all, nothing like that had ever happened before. It was simply an unbelievable vision. And even after it was confirmed as Seghva, I remember waking up and hoping it was all a bad dream."

"You aren't sorry it happened, though, are you, Telesina?" asked Marie.

"No," he answered quickly. "Not even that it happened again. I wouldn't have it any other way. But if you could only imagine the fear your fathers and I felt before he came. Even knowing the Seghva didn't ease the fear."

Their conversation lagged for a few moments, each deep in thought about the changes of the last ten years. Thomas absentmindedly played with his moustache, and then smiled as he realized that it, too, was one of the changes: He was the first Seer since the Old Ones to have one. Actually, the Old Ones also wore full beards, but even Thomas, with all his radical ideas, slang expressions and non-conformist nature, wasn't ready to go so far as to wear a beard. Maybe someday his son... His thoughts were interrupted by Marie, who rather impatiently asked, "Where are they?"

As if in answer to her question, the door to the Hall of Seers opened, and two women emerged: Gina Megan, wife of Seer Thomas, and Patty Furth, wife of Seer Marie. "C'mon, kids," Gina called over her shoulder. "We'll be late."

A boy of about five years appeared and held the door for his younger sister. And, true to a little boy's nature, he closed it just as she reached it. "Mom!" the girl screamed.

"Timmy," Gina said, "you open that door and apologize to your sister." These were future Seer Timothy, eldest child of Seer Thomas and Gina, and his sister Solana, designated successor to Seer Marie, and therefore, also a future Seer.

"Where are my two?" Telesina asked Timmy, who was holding the door closed so his sister couldn't get out.

"They left ages ago," the boy answered, followed by an "ow!" as his father swatted his rear-end to ensure compliance with Gina's instructions.

"Are they going to meet us there?" the old Seer asked. Timmy nodded. "I wish they wouldn't do that," Telesina said, mostly to himself. "I hate going to these things alone." Since his wife, Shalana Tey, sister of the Vicar's wife Sandra, had passed away more than fifteen years ago, Telesina had tried to be both father and mother to his two daughters, future Seer Savah, and her sister Serena, now both over thirty. Telesina himself was almost ninety, and It wouldn't be long he knew until Savah would take his place.

Michael London, now thirty-six and graying at the temples, stood behind a podium on the auditorium stage. Behind him sat Hartas, Laura, the Seers, Vicar Chelwith, Mrs. Enore, and, of course, Mrs. Bolan. The room was dark, and although he knew the room was full, he couldn't see any of the faces.

The celebration was in honor of the tenth anniversary of his arrival Inside. His mind went back to that awful night, when the whole world seemed to torment him: *"Jeremy's dead."* He heard the sound in his mind as if it was just yesterday. Jeremy… He remembered the dream with Seer Marcus, and he remembered what Jeremy had said, "You'll think of me from time to time. And when you do, I won't be far." A warm feeling rushed over him, like a tropical wind, and it brought tears to his eyes. He knew it was Jeremy. Michael turned to look at Hartas. He seemed so much like Jeremy, almost as if they were the same person.

Hartas, seeing the tears, whispered, "What is it?"

Michael smiled and whispered back, "I love you, Hartas." Turning once again to the audience shrouded in darkness, he began reading from his prepared speech. "Ladies and Gentlemen…" Looking up, he paused. "No," he said, putting down the papers. "My friends. My friends and my family."

Later that night, Michael and Laura were out walking on the village green. They found themselves at the dock, looking at the slahm bus that had brought them to this place years ago.

"Michael," Laura said, piercing the silence of the night, "What is this? What am I feeling?"

"It's what makes Inside special," he answered.

"But what is it?" she persisted. "I can't find the word for it."

"That's because there isn't one," he said, "at least not in English. When I first arrived, I thought the word was 'Utopia.' I thought I'd found paradise. But I kept finding holes in it: The poverty of the east village. And death: The death of Melfina, the death of Mr. Grae, the death of Harmor, and Tom and Barbara's baby. And then Ms. Shea. There were still problems, still troubles, still tragedies. It wasn't paradise. It wasn't Utopia."

"Then there isn't a word for it?" Laura asked.

"Sure there is," he said. "And the Seers told us the word our first day here. Turn around and look," he said, pointing toward the Hall of Seers, the Town Hall, the bank, barely visible in the dim light of the street lamps. "Look," he said again, pointing toward the houses on Main Street, across the green. "Can't you see it?" he asked, his voice cracking with emotion. "It's everywhere! Don't you see? They told us there was no English word for it. It isn't Utopia! It isn't paradise! It's just... knowing that everything is the way it's supposed to be. Look at the village: Can't you see it? It's as if it were written on every brick, on every piece of wood, on every shingle, on every blade of grass. It's as if all of Inside, the houses, the streets, the stream, are alive. They're all saying it: Can't you hear them? It's not paradise, Laura, it's Seghva!"

Bill Carey is a native of Brooklyn, NY and a graduate of Galway High School, Galway, NY. He has authored books on various topics, including Apostolic Doctrine, the nature of the Godhead, LGBT Christians, a children's book, a poetry book, and a modern English translation of the New Testament.

He currently lives in Ferndale, MI with his partner, Larry